C000064548

Deadly Carnage

When the train carrying him to prison is derailed, Confederate prisoner-of-war Jeff Kyle is surprised when a Yankee sergeant helps him escape. However, the sergeant is Confederate scout Mike Avison in disguise. Together, the two hatch a plan to escape to freedom, but fate intervenes in the shape of Clara Marston, who has in her possession a key to a mysterious deposit box in a bank in Independence, which she believes will make her fortune. Soon the three are joined on their journey by widowed homesteader Pollyanna Cooper, and so begins a journey full of peril and intrigue.

Deadly Carnage

Edwin Derek

A Black Horse Western

ROBERT HALE

© Edwin Derek 2019
First published in Great Britain 2019

ISBN 978-0-7198-2952-9

The Crowood Press
The Stable Block
Crowood Lane
Ramsbury
Marlborough
Wiltshire SN8 2HR

www.bhwesterns.com

Robert Hale is an imprint
of The Crowood Press

CHAPTER ONE

WRECK OF THE OLD NUMBER TEN

After the long drought, came the tornado, the most violent twister the area had seen for many years. Next came thunder, lightning and then rain. Not ordinary rain. It teemed down for hours, turning dust into mud and mud into slime that oozed across railway tracks, making them dangerously greasy.

These particular rail tracks were vital to the Yankees since south-bound trains used them to deliver supplies and munitions for the Union's last great assault against the Confederate Army. North-bound trains mainly ferried captured Reb soldiers to Union prison camps.

One such north-bound train was pulled by locomotive Number Ten. Built by the renowned Rogers Company to a design known throughout the railway world as *The American Type*, Number Ten had once been a fine passenger locomotive. Unfortunately, due to the Civil War its maintenance had too often been neglected, as indicated by its rust-stained boiler and the hissing white steam escaping from its leaking valve glands.

Worse still, the thunderous roar of its exhaust and the thick black smoke belching out of its funnel indicated to those who knew about such things that the locomotive was being driven to its absolute limit. Nevertheless, it still struggled to climb the long gradient leading to the only bridge for many a mile that crossed the fast-flowing river swollen to almost flooding point by the tempestuous storm.

Then, just as it seemed that Number Ten would reached the top of the gradient, its four large driving wheels began to spin wildly on the greasy rails. The engineer responded by closing the regulator, thereby reducing the flow of steam from the boiler to the steam chest. In turn this reduced the steam available to drive Number Ten's pistons. As a result, its big driving wheels stopped spinning but as the steam escaping from its valve glands began to disappear the locomotive's forward momentum was reduced to a mere crawl.

Even when the engineer began to reopen the regulator Number Ten struggled to pick up any speed. This was hardly surprising since it was a lightweight express originally designed to haul no more than five passenger coaches. This day it hauled no fewer than three coaches and seven heavily laden ancient freight cars, each of the latter crammed full of Reb prisoners and their guards. Consequently, each freight car was much heavier than a normal passenger coach.

The leading portion of Number Ten's first coach

carried a small number of blue-coated Yankee officers, while the rest of it had been altered to contain most of their sleeping quarters. The second coach was packed with Yankee troops returning from the front, no sleeping accommodation for them; the third had been converted to carry the officers' horses.

Heavily armed blue uniformed troops standing on top of every carriage and freight car acted as lookouts. However, there was virtually no chance of the manacled prisoners escaping from the moving train and the Confederates were all but defeated, their surrender being expected within the next few weeks. Consequently, the guards were all relaxed, paying scant regard to their duties.

Getting this train and its prisoners to its destination was the responsibility of the locomotive's engineer, not the Union officers or their troops. The engineer was concerned that by closing the regulator to stop the driving wheels spinning the overloaded Number Ten would not have sufficient steam left to reach the summit of the gradient, and he spoke sharply to his fireman.

'Bend your back, Tom. Pile on more wood before we run out of steam,' he ordered.

The fireman redoubled his efforts but there was little improvement to show for his extra work and due to the leaking glands the boiler pressure continued to fall. Then, just as it seemed Number Ten would come to a standstill, she lurched violently; her large driving wheels again spinning viciously on the slimy rails.

Caught by surprise, the engineer was unable to keep his balance, staggered across the locomotive's cab and then crashed into the wood piled high in the tender. No longer a young man, the force of the impact severely winded him and he collapsed in a heap on the viciously vibrating iron floor of his cab. His young fireman fared even worse. He was knocked out.

Weakened by years of poor maintenance the old and rusty coupling of the leading freight car was unable to withstand the uneven forces generated by Number Ten's viciously spinning driving wheels; it snapped and then parted company from those of the third carriage.

Freed of more than half their load, the locomotive's four coupled driving wheels suddenly stopped spinning and gripped the slimy rails. Like a bucking bronco, the locomotive and the three remaining coaches leapt forward. It was little short of a miracle that they were not derailed as they topped the gradient's summit and then clattered across the large trestle bridge at an ever increasing speed.

Taken completely unawares by the violence of the acceleration, most of the troops were flung off the top of the freight cars like rag dolls. Whilst several were killed by the severity of their fall most were only injured. Events were to prove they were the lucky ones.

Belatedly, the fireman's hard work resulted in a rise in steam pressure in the boiler. But there was nobody at Number Ten's controls to close her regulator. Worse still, there was a downward gradient at the far end of the bridge so she continued to pick up speed, leaving the uncoupled freight cars far behind. They slowly ground to a halt, still on the gradient, just short of the bridge, but they did not remain stationary for long.

Almost imperceptibly, the freight cars began to inch backwards down the gradient, gradually gathering momentum, and they were soon travelling backwards at an ever increasing speed, the hapless prisoners and the soldiers guarding them trapped inside.

Ever quicker, the freight cars sped back down the gradient until they were travelling far too quickly to negotiate the bend at the bottom of it. The leading freight car jumped the rails then, one after the other, the others followed, each violently ramming into the one in front of it. The noise of splintering wood intermingling with the cries of the severely maimed and dying was horrific.

Bodies, some manacled together by leg irons as in a chain gang, others with their hands handcuffed behind their backs, lay strewn among the wreckage. It seemed nobody could have lived through the crash yet a handful of prisoners had not only survived but had managed to do so without the slightest scratch.

Although badly shaken, the survivors began to make good their escape by heading towards the river. Unfortunately, as their hands were handcuffed behind them their progress was slow; too slow for the bottom of the gradient was almost two miles from the river bank.

Although he had been thrown clear of the wreckage, one prisoner could not join the escapees. No ordinary prisoner, he alone had been handcuffed to a Yankee officer. Unfortunately for the Yankee officer, his neck had been broken by the force of his landing. The prisoner, also an officer but dressed in grey, had been far luckier; he had landed in a bush stout enough to break his fall.

The Confederate lieutenant searched through the

Yankee officer's pockets until he found the keys for his handcuffs and then quickly freed himself. Yet he did not try to escape. Instead, he searched the dead officer's pockets until he found the papers he was looking for: a warrant covering his transfer north and authorizing his public hanging. It had been signed by General Grant, the overall leader of the entire Union forces. The young officer was about to put it in his tunic pocket when he was interrupted.

'I'll take that!'

It was a Yankee sergeant who, in spite of the wreckage, had moved so silently the Reb lieutenant had not detected his approach. The sergeant's right hand was outstretched to receive the warrant but in his left hand was a six-gun, its unusual brass barrel glinting brightly in the after-storm sunlight. Tucked into his trousers, most un-cavalry like, was a second more normal six-gun, a .44 calibre Army Colt. The Reb officer handed over the warrant. Caught unawares, there was nothing else he could do.

'Lieutenant Jefferson Kyle, of the 43rd Virginian Irregulars,' read the sergeant out loud.

'Yes, I am,' admitted the young lieutenant.

'So one of the Grey Fox's invincible officers actually got caught. How come?' asked the sergeant.

'I was riding with General Moseby on a raid to get supplies and ammunition when my horse got shot from under me. The fall knocked me out. When I came to I was surrounded by Union troopers. Not that it's any of your business,' retorted the lieutenant defiantly.

Universally known as the Grey Fox, General Moseby was the leader of the highly successful Partisan army known as the 43rd Virginia Irregulars. Nicknamed Moseby's Confederacy, they had been a top-notch cavalry outfit. Indeed, many senior officers of the Union Army rated them the best cavalry army of the war. And with good cause, for although always heavily outnumbered, they had wreaked havoc with their hit and run raids, during which they had consistently outwitted and outridden General Sheridan's mighty Union Army as they marched through the Shenandoah Valley.

Nevertheless, their undoubted success, which had been described by some as an irritant and likened to a mosquito biting a dog, was not enough to change the outcome of the war. Consequently a warrant authorizing death sentences for Moseby and his officers had been issued; one of the officers named on the warrant was Lieutenant Jefferson Kyle. However, to his friends he was always known as Jeff.

'None of my business, you say. Well. Since there's a noose waiting for you back east, you had better have this,' said the sergeant grinning broadly as he handed his Army Colt six-gun to the astonished lieutenant.

'Who are you?' gasped Jeff Kyle.

'Mike Avison, formerly chief scout to Jeb Stuart, the best cavalry officer in the main Confederate Army. That is, until he got himself killed. After that there didn't seem much point in staying on. I sort of retired myself and was making my way back to Texas when I ran into a troop of Yankee Cavalry and got caught like a chicken in a coop. Thought I was going to finish the War in a Yankee prison until this train crash.'

Jeb Stuart was the legendary cavalry commander who

11

had repeatedly outflanked and literally run rings around General McClellan's mighty Union Army of the Potomac. Abraham Lincoln had sacked McClellan for the debacle. Then, unfortunately for the Confederates, Lincoln appointed the extremely able Grant to replace him.

'So how come you're wearing a Yankee uniform?' asked the young lieutenant.

'I'd love to tell you my life story, boy, but what about escaping first? Can you swim? I mean swim very, very well.'

'Yes. Like a fish. I was born in Reedville, near Chesapeake Bay. They say I could swim before I could ride and I could ride before I could walk.'

'Good. What say we make for the river before what's left of that damned Yankee train returns with the rest of the Union soldiers on board? Then, sir, if you are as good a swimmer as you say you are, I'll show you how to escape from these damned Yankees.'

'Fine, sergeant, but calling me sir would be a bit of a giveaway if we are ever overheard. To hell with Army protocol, the war's almost over; my friends call me Jeff.'

CHAPTER TWO

DANGEROUS WATERS

The locomotive's engineer recovered from his fall and brought Number Ten to a stop. He had no need to inspect the train behind him; his experience taught him that it had broken into two. He could deal with that later; the first priority was to tend to Tom, his injured fireman.

But the engineer was no nursemaid. So instead, he clambered over the wood in the tender until he reached the top of the water tank. He undid its large filler cap and inserted the crude depth gauge. It was nothing more than a graded rod with a small pail attached to the end of it. Having filled the pail with water, he pulled it out of the water tank, closed its cover and detached the pail. Then, he carefully clambered back over the wood in the tender and into the locomotive's cab, taking care not to spill the water. Next, he emptied the contents of the pail over his

13

still unconscious fireman. The deluge of cold water worked wonders and Tom recovered consciousness almost immediately.

Suddenly a Yankee officer poked his head into Number Ten's cab and haughtily introduced himself.

'I'm Lieutenant Brannon. You are to reverse this train immediately and proceed down the track with all haste. We must recover the freight cars before any of the prisoners escape.'

'Lieutenant,' replied the engineer curtly, 'while I'm in charge of driving Number Ten, I'll be the judge of how fast we reverse. This type of locomotive isn't designed to go backwards quickly.'

'But it can reverse, can't it?' asked the lieutenant anxiously.

'Yes, but only very slowly and not at all until you and all the others are back in your carriages. Where the train is concerned, I'm in charge,' retorted the engineer sharply.

Suitably abashed, Lieutenant Brannon returned to the officers' carriage. Only when the engineer was certain that all the troops were back in their carriages did he restart old Number Ten. Then, very cautiously, he reversed the train back over the bridge and down the gradient.

Since the engineer's view was blocked by the three carriages now in front of the reversing locomotive, young Tom clambered up and over the wood in Number Ten's tender until he could see over the top of the carriages. Of course, the young fireman could not see the track directly in front of them but at least he could see whether the track far ahead was clear and so prevent the train running into the freight cars.

14

Although the train gradually began to pick up speed as it proceeded down the gradient it still took several minutes before it reached the wreckage. Time Lieutenant Jeff Kyle and his new-found friend, Sergeant Mike Avison, used to get away from the wrecked freight cars.

A terrible sight greeted those on board old Number Ten as it pulled up in front of the wreckage. Bodies, some with limbs at grotesque angles, lay strewn everywhere. However, it was the fleeing prisoners that grabbed the attention of the officers in the train. As soon as it stopped, they rushed to the carriage containing the horses and ordered the surviving troops to release them.

The horses were understandably skittish. Consequently, unloading them was not an easy task. Then, they had to be calmed before they could be saddled. All of which took time. . .

In spite of his cavalry boots, which were designed for riding not running, Jeff began to catch up and then overtake the other prisoners also heading for the river; their progress severely hampered by their hands still handcuffed behind their backs.

Cunningly, Mike, wearing a Yankee uniform, dropped a few yards behind Jeff and then turned and brandished his gun at some of the prisoners they had just overtaken. The prisoners, believing Mike to be a Yankee sergeant, stopped dead in their tracks.

Mike waved to draw the attention of two mounted Yankee officers, then turned and dashed after Jeff as if he was chasing another escaping prisoner. Mike, wearing ordinary Army boots, soon began to catch up the young lieutenant. The two Yankee officers didn't follow him but rode up to the other escaping prisoners and, six-guns in hand, dismounted.

The ground began to drop down towards the river. By the time Jeff and Mike reached its bank, they were out of sight of any Yankee horsemen. But Mike knew they had only won a temporary respite. Yet he paused to take off his boots, tie them together with their laces and then put them around his neck. He instructed Jeff to do the same. Then, together, they waded into the fast-flowing river.

'Strike out for the middle, boy. Stay close, I want to see if you can swim as well as you say you can,' said Mike.

He discovered Jeff could. The current made stronger by the flood water caused by the storm held no terrors for him. Yet although the lieutenant was a very strong swimmer, Mike easily outpaced him and so was forced to dog-paddle until his younger companion caught up with him. While he waited, he took off his hat.

'Boy, can you swim underwater?'

Out of breath, Jeff could only nod yes.

'Good, when I give you the word toss your hat into the river and then swim upstream towards the rail bridge, keeping underwater as much as you can,' ordered Mike, even though Jeff was the officer.

'Up river! Against this current? Are you mad?' gasped Jeff.

'Just mad enough to escape. I'm guessing the Yankees won't bother to look upstream for prisoners. So for once in your life, take an order from an enlisted man and swim underwater as much as you can until you reach the railway bridge. Rest under it if you have to but not for too long. Then, you must keep going until the bridge is so far behind you it's out of sight. Understand?'

Again Jeff nodded his head as he too dog-paddled but, unlike Mike, the current soon began to carry him down river.

'You may be a good enough swimmer to beat the current but only if you don't try to keep up with me,' continued Mike. 'Don't worry; I'll wait for you on the river bank as soon as I've found somewhere safe. Nod again if you agree.'

Jeff did just that. Without another word, Mike released his hat and as it floated downstream, dived underwater and began to swim upstream. Jeff followed suit, not a moment too soon. He had barely disappeared from view when more prisoners reached the bank. They were not alone as not far behind them galloped several mounted officers desperate to intercept them.

Only a few of the other prisoners reached the river first but, perhaps because they were still handcuffed, they hesitated on the edge of the bank. The delay cost them dearly as two more Yankee officers soon rounded them up and escorted them back to the train without so much as a glance up the river.

A little further down the river bank another Yankee officer reined in his horse. He could not fail to see two hats floating down it and, as Mike had hoped, presumed their owners had drowned. Had he looked upriver he might have seen Jeff as he surfaced for air. Fortunately for the young lieutenant, the Yankee did not and rode back to the wrecked freight cars instead.

The strong current made it a long and hard swim to the railway bridge. Almost out of breath, Jeff was forced to

make for the bank and rest. Fortunately, the wooden railroad bridge was the usual sprawling trestle design that
towered over the river. Hidden from view under its many
wooden spars, Jeff was able to rest in comparative safety,
but he knew he could not stay there for long. He guessed
he had taken an hour or so to swim to the railway bridge,
ample time for the Yankees to regroup and ride up the
river bank to the bridge.

No riders appeared. Jeff guessed the reason the
Yankees hadn't sent a patrol along the river bank meant
that Mike's ruse with their hats had worked and that they
believed any prisoners they hadn't rounded up had
drowned. Not that there were many to round up. Most of
the Confederate prisoners had died in the wrecked freight
cars.

Knowing the troops did not have the necessary equip-
ment to give the dead a decent burial, Jeff surmised their
officers would be anxious to leave the crash site. Jeff also
believed that the Yankees would waste little time in
herding their prisoners into what was left of the train.
However, before they continued on their journey their
horses would have to be unsaddled and loaded back into
the train.

All of which would take time. However, not that much
longer than he had spent swimming to the bridge, so the
train would be crossing over the bridge sooner rather than
later. Unfortunately, Mike had been right; the towering
trestle bridge afforded a view for miles to anyone looking
out of the carriage windows as the train crossed it. So he
was certain to be seen if he continued to swim up the river.

Wearily, Jeff plunged back into the flow and then swam

to its middle, ensuring he stayed undercover of the bridge at all times. Then he dog-paddled for all he was worth and this time managed to stop the current sweeping him downstream.

It wasn't long before he heard the sound of Number Ten steaming up the gradient. With only three coaches to pull, even though they were seriously overcrowded, it was under little strain and this time made good progress up the severe gradient.

Just to be on the safe side, Jeff dived under water and remained there until, gasping for breath, he had to resurface. As he did so, the train crossed over the bridge, forcing him to dive back under the water; by the time he again resurfaced the sound of the rapidly moving train was barely audible and soon faded into nothingness.

Nevertheless, he wasn't about to take any chances and before he began to swim up the river he once again dived under, resurfacing only when he needed air. He continued the process until he realized his progress was too slow to have any chance of reaching Mike before his new-found friend tired of waiting for him. Risking being seen, he stayed on the surface and swam on as rapidly as the strong current would allow him.

As dusk fell, almost exhausted, he began to head for the bank, only to be hailed from the opposite one.

'Boy, if you had a lick of sense you'd know that's the wrong side! There's nothing over there but open grassland.'

It was Mike. Wearily, Jeff turned round and swam to the opposite bank and clambered out. Almost too tired to walk, he was only too happy to be supported by Mike, who seemed untroubled by his arduous swim. He led Jeff to a wooded dell, at the bottom of which was a most welcoming fire. Too tired and wet to wonder how Mike had managed to light it, Jeff basked in its warmth and then lay down. Although the ground was hard and his clothes were still steaming, he was asleep in seconds.

It was almost dawn when he was awoken by Mike. Yet it seemed to the young lieutenant he had only been asleep a few moments.

'Come on, boy. We gotta get out of here.'

'You're right. I guess we should put as much distance between us and the crash site as quickly as we can,' replied Jeff sleepily.

'Guess again, boy. I'm going back there right now. If you're hungry, come with me, but only if you've got a strong stomach. We got a mighty unpleasant chore to do before we can think about eating.'

Although Jeff Kyle was an officer, more used to giving orders than receiving them, he followed Mike without a second thought. Indeed, he was very hungry; he hadn't eaten since they had been herded into the freight cars more than thirty-six hours ago. Yet all thoughts of food were driven out of his head as they reached the top of the dell. The river swept around in a huge arc. In a straight line, on land the railway bridge was barely half a mile away.

CHAPTER THREE

CARNAGE

It didn't take them long to reach the place where the train had split in two. Bodies thrown off the roofs of the freight cars lay on the muddy ground. As Mike had guessed, their bodies lay exactly where they had fallen.

'This is where you earn your breakfast, boy. You got the stomach to search dead men?'

'Sure. Done it before many times. Where do you think the 43rd got its six-guns and ammo from? But only officers tote Colt pistols, soldiers carry Springfield muskets and they ain't a lick of good to us.'

'Boy, we're looking for money, ammunition and anything else we can use.'

'Since when did ordinary soldiers get paid?' replied Jeff.

During his years in Moseby's Confederacy he had never received a cent. Not that the invincible 43rd ever went short of anything. They were well supported by the civilian population. Unlike the Partisan Armies of Quantrell and then Anderson, the Irregulars only raided Yankee-held towns and had always protected Southern interests wherever and whenever they were able.

Raids on the Yankees had yielded almost everything they had needed plus several hauls of money. Jeff's own share was stashed in a derelict farm building in a remote part of the Shenandoah Valley. However, the valley had been completely overrun by Grant's Union Army. So for all the good it was going to do him his loot might as well have been stashed on the moon. As for the finances of these Union troops, Mike had the answer.

'Boy, if you had kept alert yesterday, you might have heard the Yankees bragging about being paid the day before they took up guarding the train. So get searching, and while you're about it find a Yankee uniform that fits you. If we are going to escape you've got to get out of that Reb officer's uniform.'

'If I get caught in a Yankee uniform they will shoot me as a spy,' protested Jeff.

'So don't get caught,' retorted Mike.

The search revealed little of value. In spite of Mike's earlier assurances they only found a few dollars and there wasn't a uniform that fitted Jeff. However, Mike was not about to give up.

'It's still pretty early, so if we hurry, there should be enough time to search the wreck site,' he said.

'Perhaps, but not for you. But we thank you for saving us the trouble of searching these corpses.'

Three ragged and disreputable-looking Union troopers stepped out from under the bridge, where they had been hiding Jeff neither knew nor cared. One, the speaker, had already drawn his six-gun, the right hands of the other two hovered ominously over the butt of theirs.

They had the drop on Jeff and Mike. Or they should have had. Like a flash of lightning, Mike drew, cocked his six-gun and fired in the same instant. Yet, fast as he was, Jeff beat him to it and his man was dead before Mike's bullet struck its target, the trooper holding the six-gun.

The remaining trooper drew and fired just as Jeff got off his second shot. Not used to packing a six-gun, the trooper missed. Traditionally, Union cavalry men carried sabres and muskets, only their officers toted six-guns. Jeff, on the other hand, had always carried a Colt six-gun and so didn't miss; the trooper was dead before he hit the ground.

'Damned fool,' growled Mike as he holstered his six-gun.

'Us or them?' asked Jeff as he carefully checked the bodies to ensure they were dead.

'Me for not spotting them. Some scout you must think me,' Mike said bitterly.

'I missed them, too. Fortunately, they were the fools. They had the drop on us yet they're the dead ones. Had they shot from cover instead of coming forward to gloat over us they might have lived a bit longer.'

'True, but that was some mighty fine shooting by you. Two hits with a six-gun you've never used before! Where did you learn to shoot like that?'

'Riding with Moseby. There were times when we had to use whatever six-guns we could find. We buried those of us who couldn't adapt.'

They then searched the new bodies but found nothing of interest.

'Guess they were deserters,' said Mike when they had finished.

'Seems likely,' agreed Jeff. 'Just lucky for us there were only three of them.'

'And as you said, they talked to us instead of shooting first. But how did you know I'd go for the trooper holding the gun? We could have both gone for the same man.'

'I figured since you were a scout you'd be able to handle a six-gun, so you'd go for the trooper holding the six-gun since you didn't know whether I could shoot or not.'

'I sure do now but I'd better check out the area again. We don't need any more surprises.'

Apart from dead bodies the entire area was deserted so they clambered up the railway embankment and then jogged down the tracks to the wrecked freight cars. Jeff, still in his cavalry riding boots, found it impossible to keep up with Mike. By the time he reached the derailed freight cars Mike was already amid the carnage searching through the dead bodies.

And carnage it was. There were too many bodies scattered around the wrecked freight cars to count, yet there was more than double that amount inside them.

A whoop of joy from Mike indicated that he had hit the jackpot. These soldiers had indeed received their pay and at least some of them had not had the chance to spend it. Mike not only found money; two of the soldiers he searched also carried a surprisingly large quantity of spare ammunition.

24

While Mike counted the money, more than a hundred dollars in all, Jeff searched the least damaged freight car. Least damaged on the outside maybe, yet all the unfortunate souls inside it were dead. Among the Confederate bodies were two Yankee soldiers and one, rather surprisingly, was a major; the other was a corporal. The major was about the same size as Mike but the corporal was a little heavier built than Jeff. Nevertheless, his uniform might prove to be a passable fit.

'Why couldn't the major's uniform have been the right size for me,' he grumbled out aloud, thinking how much Mike would enjoy wearing it and playing the role of a senior officer.

However, before he had time to tell Mike of his find or change into the corporal's uniform, he heard the plaintive wail of a locomotive whistle. It sounded a long way off. Even so, they couldn't make it to the river bank before it arrived. Yet there was no other escape route. Unless . . . born out of desperation, an idea suddenly came to him. But he needed to explain it to Mike if it was to work. Fortunately, the bogus Union sergeant had also heard the train whistle and rushed back to the freight car.

'Leave me here. Go and flag down the train and tell them what happened,' said Jeff.

'What good will that do?' replied Mike sceptically.

Jeff began to explain his idea.

'I'll play dead. It's not likely the troops on the train will be equipped to bury so many bodies, so I should get away with it.'

'What do I do then?' asked Mike.

'Get on the train. You're wearing a Yankee uniform so

you should be able to fool them for long enough to escape.'

Mike thought hard for a moment. Jeff's idea had some merit but it could be improved. There wasn't time to explain, so he pretended to go along with Jeff.

'Good idea. But my brass barrelled six-gun is only made in the South, so it's a dead giveaway. Swap six-guns, boy.'

Jeff did as he was bid. Mike proffered his six-gun, butt forward. However, as Jeff reached out, Mike swung his arm and struck the lieutenant a sharp blow on the head. Jeff went down as if he had been poleaxed.

'Playing dead won't do, boy. They are bound to search through the bodies. Trust me, your death warrant is our ticket to freedom.'

Jeff did not answer; he couldn't for he was out cold.

Calmly, Mike began to search the two dead Yankees. On the major's body he found a letter addressed to Major Hancock and a movement pass; a wallet with a considerable sum of money in it, at least as much as he had already collected. He also found several documents and a key. There was also a bill of sale for two horses. It seemed they had belonged to the dead Major Hancock rather than the Yankee Army.

The date of their shipment suggested the horses might be on the train he had just heard whistling. But why? What had the major been up to? Not Army business for sure. The train whistled again. It sounded a little nearer this time so he stuffed the money into his wallet and crammed the documents into his tunic. Without thinking, he also picked up the key and absent-mindedly put it into his pocket.

He bent down and searched the corporal's body. Almost at once he found what he was looking for; a pair of handcuffs and a set of keys to go with them. He quickly handcuffed the still unconscious Jeff and was about to stuff the keys into his pocket when another idea struck him.

But was there enough time? He looked outside the freight car and was pleasantly surprised to see the locomotive was still a long way off. It must have been moving very slowly for it still seemed to be little more than a black dot swathed in white smoke.

Mike turned back into the freight car, and stripped. Dressed only in long johns, he removed the major's uniform and exchanged it for his sergeant's uniform, remembering to transfer his wallet and the other documents as he did so. The new uniform was such a good fit it might have been made for him.

'A sergeant yesterday, a major today. Promotion is mighty quick in the Yankee Army,' he said chuckling to himself as he stepped out of the freight car and strode towards the oncoming train.

There was no need to flag it down as it proved to be a heavily laden, slow-moving freight train. The locomotive, still shrouded in steam, was crawling along at a snail's place. So it was still a couple of minutes before it pulled up, hissing and leaking steam, some thirty yards short of the wreckage.

A young-looking officer jumped down from the cab and marched through the steam towards Mike. He stopped and saluted smartly. His face turned ashen as he surveyed the carnage.

Mike returned the salute. This is going to work, he thought to himself, especially if I don't give this Yankee lieutenant time to think.

'I'm Major Hancock, here are my papers,' he said, passing the warrant for Lieutenant Kyle to the Yankee lieutenant.

Although the war was four years old, it seemed likely that this young officer had not yet seen any war action for he was clearly affected by the carnage all around him. So much so, he barely glanced at the warrant before handing it back to Mike.

'That seems in order, sir. As you are the senior officer, I place my men and myself under your command and respectfully await your orders.'

Mike chuckled inwardly; changing into the major's uniform was already paying big dividends. As a sergeant, he would have had to follow orders instead of giving them.

'What's your current assignment, lieutenant?' he asked in what he hoped was an authoritative tone.

'Riding guard to this freight train, sir. It's carrying cattle for the eastern market and a few horses. Headquarters received information that it was likely to be a raided but it seems the Rebs chose your train to attack rather than ours. I guess they were trying to free your prisoners.'

Mike nodded his head as if in agreement. The lieutenant's assumption would buy him precious time. Of course, as soon as the lieutenant's troops had examined the bodies they would realize their deaths were the result of a train crash rather than the bullets of the enemy. By that time, however, he intended that he and Lieutenant Kyle would be long gone.

Mike reached into his pocket and pulled out the documents relating to the real Hancock's horses.

'Lieutenant, I believe your train is carrying a couple of my own steeds. Would you care to have them unloaded?'

Before the Yankee lieutenant could reply they were interrupted by the arrival of the freight locomotive's engineer.

'This is a damned fine mess,' he said. 'We can't go on and we can't risk going back in case we run into an unscheduled train. You never can tell what the Army's going to do next.'

'Have your men stand guard over the train, lieutenant. Then break out my horses and one other horse. Choose your best rider. I'll write a dispatch to headquarters apprising them of the situation and ask them to send assistance.'

'You're leaving, sir?' queried the lieutenant.

'Yes, my orders are clear. I'm escorting a rather special prisoner and my orders are to get him to Washington with all due dispatch whatever else happens. So you will take charge here until HQ relieves you. Keep your men on alert; remember there may still be Rebs about.'

'Yes sir. Will you need any assistance with your prisoner?'

'No. I left him unconscious and handcuffed. Get your men deployed, lieutenant.'

With that Mike turned around and walked briskly back to the wrecked freight car to find that Jeff had recovered but was still groggy. Seeing Mike bedecked in a major's uniform confused him still further.

'Don't talk,' snapped Mike. 'There are at least two dozen Yankee soldiers outside but they are our way out of here.'

'Yankees help us! Have you gone mad?' protested Jeff.

'Listen. I'm now Major Hancock and you are still Kyle, but you are now my prisoner. I'm supposed to be taking you to Washington, where you're due to hang. Got that?'

'Yes, but get me out of these handcuffs.'

'Not until we're out of here. In the meantime, find me some paper; I've a dispatch to write.'

A few minutes later, Mike and the still handcuffed Jeff rode away from the train carnage. Their steeds had pure white bodies covered with patches. The patches on Mike's steed were all black; back east this combination was usually referred to as piebald. The patches on Jeff's steed were a glorious golden brown; a combination known as skewbald. However, whether they had brown or black patches, they were both a unique breed of horse called pinto, although in Texas they were more usually called paints.

Although not popular among cowboys, many of whom considered them to be too flashy; they were highly prized by all the nomadic warrior Indian tribes, especially the Sioux, and were often the mounts of chiefs. Perhaps that was the real reason most cowboys shunned them.

They were, however, extremely fashionable back east, where they were always in great demand. Consequently, a well-defined pinto or paint was usually worth several times more than a mustang. Possibly that was why the real Major Hancock had arranged to have these two shipped back east. Unfortunately, these stunning-looking steeds were about as conspicuous as it was possible to get and would be bound to attract comment wherever they rode.

None of which bothered Mike in the least. He had

more pressing problems on his mind, the most important of which was how long would it be before the Yankee lieutenant realized he had been duped? What would he do then? Would he still guard the freight train until reinforcements arrived or would he send at least some of his men after them? Mike didn't know so he discussed the matter with Jeff, now free of his handcuffs.

In spite of the desperate need to put as much distance between them and the soldiers guarding the trains, once out of sight they reined in their steeds and continued at little more than walking pace. In any case, in order to back up Mike's story he was taking his prisoner to Washington, they were heading north. So every stride was taking them further away from safety and deeper into enemy-held territory.

Nevertheless, they rode steadily northwards along the river bank until nightfall and then camped. Unfortunately, they still had no food; neither had eaten for almost three days.

'God, I'm hungry and those damned handcuffs have rubbed my wrists raw,' complained Jeff.

'Better sore wrists than a rope round your neck, boy. But you got a point. We need food and we can't keep up this deception much longer. It's got us this far but as you're the real officer, it's time for you to come up with the next part of the escape plan.'

'Let me sleep on it. Apart from anything else, I can't think straight after that wallop you gave me.'

'All part of the service,' chuckled Mike as he unsaddled his paint.

*

Even hungrier, Jeff woke early. Whether it was from lack of food or the blow he had received from Mike's six-gun, he couldn't think straight. So he made his way down to the river, stripped and then plunged in. The water was as cold as the last time but at least it cleared his head and focused his mind, which was the point of the exercise. By the time he returned to the bank he had formulated not one but a series of plans.

'Thought you would have had enough swimming to last a lifetime. In any case, you're supposed to be my prisoner. Bathing on your own and then parading on the bank dressed in a Confederate uniform is a bit of a giveaway,' growled Mike.

'Stop worrying, I made sure nobody saw me. Now listen up, I've worked out the plan you asked for.'

CHAPTER FOUR

GUN DUEL IN THE DARK

Storm clouds flitted across the moon as it illuminated the writing on the sign in front of Jeff Kyle.

CLANTONVILLE
Population 1,003

Several days had passed since he had outlined his plan to Mike. Long days during which they had continued north-west instead of heading south for the safety of Confederate-held territory. They had almost lost count of the days since they had last eaten but when fighting for the South such hardships were not that unusual. Jeff's goal was to locate a town and search for food. Under Moseby's leadership he had become expert in foraging in many an unknown town. So he had left Mike at their campsite, or

33

so he thought.

Still in his Reb uniform, he had arrived in Clantonville a little after dusk. Finding a disused picket about half a mile outside the town limits, he had tethered his paint and then waited patiently until most of its citizens had gone to bed. Only then did he venture into the town.

A howling dog suddenly broke the night's silence and Jeff's train of thought. The dog ceased howling. Nothing else stirred, not too surprising since it was long past midnight. After a few moments he continued towards the centre of the little town, taking care not to be seen by any late-night reveller. He was hoping to find an open window he could climb through and search for food. If he got lucky he might also find some civilian clothes that fit him.

He was more than halfway down a pleasant back lane that led into what he guessed to be the town's high street when he heard the sound of raised voices and then female laughter. The sounds were coming from the high street but the voices were coming towards him. Would their owners continue along the high street or turn into the back lane? Jeff's right hand automatically reached for his brass barrelled six-gun but then stopped. Gunshots might awaken half the town, besides there was a least one woman in the group.

Strangely, a few yards ahead of Jeff, parked in front of a large town house, was a stagecoach. Of course, at this late hour it didn't have any horses attached to it. So he opened its door and climbed into its dark interior.

Not a second too soon, for as he did so the clouds that had intermittently hidden the moon for most of the night rolled by and the lane was suddenly bathed in bright moonlight. Fortunately, it was not quite strong enough to illuminate the interior of the stagecoach, which was just as well because the owners of the voices turned into the back lane. As they approached the stagecoach Jeff began to hear what they were saying. Although he could not see he could tell that only two people approached. One, a female, seemed in high spirits; the other was a man who seemed to have things on his mind that precluded him from looking out for strangers.

'Quiet my dear, we don't want to disturb my neighbours, do we?' said the man.

'No, that wouldn't do at all, would it? They might tell your wife. Where is she anyway?' asked the girl.

'Gone to visit her sister, she won't be back until tomorrow afternoon. She's coming back on the stage.'

'That gives us plenty of time, you naughty old mayor,' giggled the female. When she laughed, she sounded quite young.

'Time for what dear?' asked the man with feigned innocence.

'You had better know for what!' The woman giggled again as she continued. 'I hope, Mr Mayor, you haven't dragged me out of the saloon just for a chat.'

By this time, the couple were level with the stagecoach. But instead of passing it they turned and headed towards the big town house. Jeff shrank back into the shadows of the stagecoach. Again there was no need; the man was too preoccupied with his surprisingly young companion. In the moonlight Jess could see that she was dressed in a daring, low-cut dress of a style typically worn by saloon girls, although she seemed to be little more than sixteen.

The man, on the other hand, was quite portly, very well dressed and almost certainly in his late forties.

As they entered the big house, Jeff heard the girl ask, 'Why is there a stagecoach outside your house, Mr Mayor?'

'It's part of a surprise for my wife, my dear.' he replied. 'Tomorrow, I'm going to collect her from the station in the stagecoach. When we return home, she's going to find the house full of our friends. I'm throwing a little party to mark her return. But tonight, it will be just the two of us.'

'Come on then. No more talking, let's go inside,' said the girl. Even though it was long past midnight, she appeared eager to go into the empty house. She grabbed the mayor and arm-in-arm they walked hurriedly up its path. He opened the front door and a few seconds later the front room of the house was flooded in light from an oil lamp. Apart from illuminating the parlour, its rays were strong enough to illuminate the street, so Jeff was forced to remain inside the stagecoach.

If the mayor had been bothered about the noise the couple were making as he approached his house, he didn't appear to care what any passer-by could see through his window. He had scarcely put the lamp down on the table when he was involved in a passionate embrace with the girl. An embrace that the girl returned with interest.

On the table behind the lamp was a cold sliced chicken and some cheese. Jeff looked at the food with longing; he had not eaten for several days. The food, however, held little interest for the couple. A hunger of a very different kind consumed them as the girl slipped out of her dress. Then, carrying the lighted lamp, they left the parlour. A few moments later, the light reappeared in the unshuttered window of the front bedroom. The lane was still deserted, which was fortunate for the mayor because the girl began to remove the rest of her clothes. Only when she was completely naked did she notice the open shutters. The mayor, whose attention had been solely focused on the girl as she removed her clothes, dashed across the bedroom and slammed them shut.

Although there had been several saloon girls in his past, Jeff had never seen one quite so young or so obviously willing to make love. He might have been envious of the mayor had his rumbling stomach not forcibly reminded him how hungry he was. It was time to forget the saloon girl and put the main part of his plan into operation. However, in order to move silently he first removed his riding boots and then put them on the seat facing him.

The bedroom shutters greatly diminished the light emitting from the bedroom, nevertheless there was just enough reaching the street to make up for the disappearance of the moon behind yet another series of clouds. Treading carefully so as to avoid any stones hurting his unshod feet, Jeff made his way up to the house and pushed on its door. It swung open. As he had hoped, the couple had been too preoccupied with each other to bother to lock it. Taking great care, he entered the house and quietly closed the door.

Once again, caution was unnecessary. The groaning bedsprings indicated the girl's extraordinary enthusiasm extended to her love making; her loud groans and even louder shouts of exultation would have drowned out a herd of buffaloes stampeding through the parlour.

Nevertheless, Jeff had a problem. He could see

absolutely nothing as he entered the unlit parlour. Even the wildest love making antics of the couple upstairs would not be enough to drown out the sound of anything he sent crashing if he stumbled in the inky darkness.

He turned his attention to the kitchen. As he entered it the moon shone through a patch in the clouds, briefly giving enough light to see by. Jeff gasped at the massive size of the kitchen and drooled over the vast spread of food before him. It seemed that the mayor did indeed intend to throw a surprise party tomorrow to mark the return of his wife. It also seemed that the chicken and ham in the parlour had only been intended as an accompaniment for the mayor's midnight romp with the young saloon girl. However, their passion had clearly overcome their hunger. Indeed, the saloon girl's moans of pleasure penetrated into the kitchen, even though its door was firmly shut. But her state of seemingly unbridled ecstasy couldn't last. Jeff had to hurry.

Two enormous turkeys, a whole side of cooked beef, two large joints of cold pork and several joints of gammon were crammed on to the large kitchen table. But it didn't end there. A side table was laden with so many cooked chickens that he didn't have time to count them. Strangely, on the kitchen dresser there were several large bowls full of hard-boiled eggs.

The noise from the bedsprings and the girl's loud moans suddenly ceased. The house became silent, but not for long. Raised voices coming from the bedroom suggested an argument had broken out between the lovers. With the kitchen door closed, Jeff could only make out a few words but heard enough to suggest the girl was demanding money for staying for the rest of the night. The mayor, having got his way with her for nothing, seemed reluctant to pay for an encore.

Jeff looked around the kitchen. His mind had been so focused on finding food he had not given any thought to how he was going to get it back to their camp. So he rifled through the dressers drawers until he found an old table-cloth, which he immediately spread out on the floor.

The food on the main table would definitely be missed, so he helped himself to three roast chickens and a small bacon joint on the side table. There was so much food piled high on it he thought they might not be missed. The same applied to the hard-boiled eggs, so he picked up as many as he could carry. Indeed, there was so much food in the kitchen he felt he could have taken twice as much without it being noticed.

Jeff placed all the food he had taken in the centre of the tablecloth, then grabbed hold of its four corners, drew them together over the food and then knotted all four together, thus transforming the tablecloth into a usable sack. He slung it over his shoulder and let himself out. Then, very carefully for he was still only wearing socks, he made his way back to the stagecoach in order to retrieve his boots. He climbed into it and quietly shut its door behind him.

He wasn't a second too soon, for just as he sat down the door of the mayor's house burst open to reveal the young saloon girl, almost naked. In spite of her scanty apparel she hurried down the street, muttering such phrases as 'rotten miser, dirty skinflint' and exclaiming, 'Wait till your wife gets back tomorrow, that party won't be the only surprise she gets, I'll see to that!'

Jeff donned his boots and then waited until he was sure nobody had been alerted by the girl's noisy departure. Then he slipped out of the stagecoach and started to make his way out of town. As he did so, the moon again escaped from its cloud cover just in time to stop him running into two men. Glinting in the moonlight, a star on the chest of one of them indicated that he was a lawman. Of course, neither of them saw Jeff. He had become too proficient in the art of silent night raiding during the time he had served in the 43rd Irregulars to be caught out in the open. In any case, another belt of clouds soon obscured the moon.

Hidden in the shadows, Jeff carefully lowered the food he was carrying to the ground and then watched the men as they stopped in mid-stride and each lit a cigarette.

'Another quiet patrol,' said the deputy.

'Quiet as the grave. Wouldn't think that we were still at war,' replied the other man.

'Jed, if the rumours are to believed, it won't last much longer,' said the deputy.

'Even so, patrolling a town as quiet as the grave is a damned sight better than doing sentry duty on the battle-front.'

'Too right,' agreed the deputy. 'The only thing I got out of the war was a bust-up leg. After I was discharged I even had to buy civilian clothes out of back pay. By the time I'd bought a horse and saddle I was almost broke.'

'Tough luck. But the war has had its uses. When it's over I guess I'll have to go back to being a drifter. In peacetime things will get even quieter in Clantonville so there will be little need of a deputy and no need at all of auxiliary lawmen.'

'Right again, Jed, unless I can get enough dirt on the mayor to get him to persuade the town committee to fire the sheriff. In any case, our sheriff is more interested in his clandestine business ventures than upholding the law. So my guess is that it wouldn't take much to persuade the town committee to fire him. They said as much in the meeting this afternoon. So, if I can get enough incriminating evidence against the mayor he will have to get me elected sheriff. I will only accept on the condition they make you my full-time deputy.'

'Sounds good, if you can pull it off but, if I'm not being too nosey, what's the pay for a deputy?' asked Jed.

'Reckon the sheriff gets no more than fifty dollars a month. Me, I get thirty.'

'That's no more than a cowboy on a trail drive,' exclaimed Jed. He sounded disappointed.

'But I get a soft warm bed every night, breakfast each morning and powder and shot to roll my own ammunition free. But that's nothing to the perks our sheriff gets. Now I ain't greedy like him. Help me out now and when we're elected I'll see you get your fair share of whatever's going. I'm pretty sure the sheriff has got several back-handed deals on the go, one of which I'll gladly share with you each week.'

'Which one?' asked Jed eagerly.

'As part of the deal to turning a blind eye to the rigged gambling tables and marked playing cards in the Alhambra saloon he gets a backhander, although as yet I don't know how much. I hope to find that out tonight.

'Only part of the deal?' What else does the mayor get?' asked Jed.

'Yes, the best part of his deal is that each and every week he gets a couple of saloon girls all night for free. So that's one for me and the other will be yours.'

'Saloon girls for free!' exclaimed Jed loudly. 'In that case, count me in. But what dirt have you got on the mayor?'

'Plenty, Jed. But I need written proof. I paid one of the saloon girls to keep him busy for most of the night so I can snoop around his private office. So you finish this patrol on your own while I do the snooping.'

'I know about his personal office. It's tucked away behind the main stables. I guess that's where he entertains the girls. Getting in to it shouldn't be a problem but I happen to know that the mayor keeps his personal accounts and all the other important stuff locked away in his big old safe,' protested Jed.

'No problem when you got the safe keys,' chuckled the deputy.

'The sheriff never lets them out of his sight. How did you get them without him knowing?' asked Jed.

'My friend from the saloon kept him occupied while I made a copy, but never you mind about that. All you need to know is that I've got the keys to the safe,' chuckled the deputy. 'Now, Jed, there's a lot more involved than sleeping with a saloon girl every week. Some of the work might be dangerous if my other information is correct, so are you up for it?'

'Sure. Like I said, count me in. Now, I ain't in a hurry, so take your time to get what you need from the mayor's private office while I finish the round. As there's no prisoners to guard in the sheriff's office the janitor went home hours ago. So when I've done I'll brew us some fresh coffee.'

Without another word, the deputy left. Jeff noticed that he walked not with a limp but stiff legged; his left leg did not bend at the knee. Jed, however, and much to Jeff's concern, stayed where he was and lit another cigarette. Jeff was right to be concerned. The breeze finally blew the last of the clouds away and his hiding place was suddenly illuminated by moonlight. There was nothing he could do; by some mischance Jed was looking straight at him.

'Who the hell are you?' snarled Jed as he reached for his six-gun. He was quick, very quick, but speed alone is never enough. Jed got his shot in first but it was wide of its intended target. Jeff's shot wasn't. It struck Jed full in the chest; the violence of the impact knocked him backwards. By the time he hit the road he was already dead.

Unused to being outdrawn, Jeff was shaken, even though he had not been hit. But the shots might have been heard so there was no time to dwell on his lucky escape. Instead, he threw caution to the wind and raced back to the picket where he had tethered his skewbald paint. However, he need not have hurried; it seemed that the citizens of Clantonville were used to late-night shootings for nobody stirred from their slumber. Indeed, nobody followed Jeff as he rode back to the camp.

He was surprised to find the camp site deserted. Mike and his paint had gone. However, apart from some hard riding Jeff had been on his feet for some hours, an especially hard chore for a former cavalry man used to riding everywhere. Besides, he was too hungry to care where Mike had gone.

He grabbed a bite to eat, then fatigue overtook him. The ground was hard but it didn't matter. Using his saddle as a pillow, he was asleep in seconds and remained sound asleep until, just past dawn, he was awakened by the sound of an approaching horse. However, although it was Mike's distinctive piebald paint, even from a distance the slight stature of its rider indicated he was not its rider. Jeff drew his brass-barrelled six-gun but did not use it. As the rider drew nearer, he gasped in amazement, simply unable to believe his eyes.

CHAPTER FIVE

AVISON'S NIGHT OUT

Mike watched Jeff ride out of their temporary camp, a secluded hollow about two hours' ride from the small town of Clantonville. The young lieutenant was still in his Reb uniform, so he guessed that Jeff would keep off the main trail and hide out near the town until its citizens had settled down to sleep. So it would not be until about midnight before he began to search the town for food and a change of clothes.

Although he had agreed to stay behind and guard the camp, Mike had no intention of doing so. He had a plan of his own, so outrageous he thought he'd better not share it with his new friend.

Unlike Jeff, there would be no sneaking around for him. His targets were also some civilian clothes and then a cooked dinner, and he knew how to get both. He waited until he was sure the young lieutenant was out of sight, then saddled up his paint and also headed for Clantonville. Far from keeping out of sight, Mike took the main trail into town and then made directly for the sheriff's office. As it was now late afternoon he was surprised to find that neither the sheriff nor his deputy were available.

'The sheriff has been away from Clantonville all day. Said he had some county business to attend to. As for his deputy, he's been closeted with the town's big wigs all afternoon,' replied the jail's janitor in response to Mike's inquiries.

'Any idea when the sheriff will be back?' asked Mike.

'Not until later this evening,' said the janitor. 'But he's always pleased to see any Union officer. Colonel O'Hallaran of the 4th Pennsylvanians often drops by. If you want to see the sheriff tonight, he normally dines at the Alhambra saloon about nine, so I guess he will be back by then.'

The layout of the Alhambra saloon was typical of many saloons Mike had been in. A single bar ran the length of one wall; behind it was a huge and equally long mirror. At the far end of the saloon was a small stage that was disappointingly empty, as were most of the gaming tables. In fact, the saloon was barely a quarter full and several saloon girls were idly gossiping for want of any customers. They glanced up as he entered but, noticing his Army uniform, looked disappointed and returned to their gossiping.

Mike had brought with him about half the money he had collected from the dead soldiers; whiskey would have been his first choice but as he hadn't eaten for days and needed to keep a clear head he settled for root beer. At least it was better than river water.

The sheriff arrived just after nine.

'We haven't met before, Major. Have you been with the 4th long?'

'No, it's a temporary assignment.' Mike replied, playing the role of Major Hancock as best as he could.

'I've been expecting Colonel O'Hallaran,' continued the sheriff.

'Kind of busy at the moment. You hear of the train crash?'

'Of course, but I understood that your colonel wasn't on it.'

'No but I was. That's why I'm on this damned fool mission.'

'What mission, Major? But wait,' the sheriff threw up his arms in mock apology, 'I'm forgetting my manners. I always eat late and I guess you haven't eaten yet. Only a matter of cooking an extra steak if you would care to join me.'

Food at last! Mike happily agreed and followed the sheriff to a private upstairs room that had been converted into a small dining room presumably for his benefit.

'You were going to tell me about your mission,' prompted the sheriff after they had sat down.

Mike, confident his deception was working perfectly, began to embellish his original story.

'I've been ordered to scout north. Firstly to check there were no Rebs in the area and secondly to ensure a prisoner called Kyle hasn't come this way. Drawn a blank in both cases, so I rode into town to ask you to keep a look out. I don't think Kyle will come this way but you never can tell, he's clever for a Reb. He used to serve in Moseby's Irregulars and they were masters at disappearing into the countryside after a raid.'

Served by one of the otherwise unoccupied saloon girls, the steak was accompanied by a rare delicacy for Mike, grilled tomatoes, and an old favourite, black-eyed peas. That was followed by apple pie and cream. Not knowing where his next meal was coming from, Mike had seconds.

He had just finished when the girl returned with an unopened bottle of whiskey and several large cigars. She gave one to Mike and then produced a silver cigar clipper from under the cleavage of her dress. She gave it to Mike. It was still quite warm. He had been happily married until his wife had died of a fever just before the beginning of the Civil War. Since then he had served in the Confederate Army and there had been little time for any other women. But now, the intimate warmth of the cigar clipper unsettled him in a way that hadn't happened in years.

'They keep a special bottle of whiskey for me, much better quality than they serve downstairs,' said the sheriff, bringing Mike back to the present.

'So tell me about the train wreck,' the sheriff asked as he poured out a second generous helping of whiskey. 'Was it the Rebs?'

'To tell the truth I don't remember too much about it,' replied Mike, making up the story as he went along. 'One second I was in the carriage, next thing I was beside the track. Must have been knocked out cold for when I came round there were bodies all round me and dozens of prisoners escaping. But there was no sign of any Rebs and you would have thought they would have moved in for the kill if they'd caused the wreck.'

'I guess you're right. Did you recapture the prisoners?'

'All bar Kyle,' replied Mike; the beginnings of another idea were beginning to come to him.

'Well that's not too bad, Major. It could have been much worse.'

'No it couldn't.' Mike reached into his tunic, pulled out Kyle's movement papers and the warrant for his execution. The sheriff studied the documents and then handed them back to Avison, who returned them to his tunic pocket.

'I'd appreciate you keeping the matter as quiet as possible, I don't want your town getting jumpy and start shooting at shadows,' Avison continued.

'Surely you don't think Kyle would have travelled this far north. Wouldn't he have headed south towards the Shenandoah Valley?'

'That would be my guess. But Colonel O'Hallaran will be held responsible if Kyle escapes and I wouldn't want to face Sheridan with the news that his prize prisoner had escaped.'

'Major, if Kyle is so important, why wasn't he hung as soon as he was caught?'

'You got me there, Sheriff. They don't tell mere majors things like that!' laughed Mike, but he was bluffing for all his worth.

The bluff seemed to at least partly convince the sheriff. Fortunately, the sudden arrival of the town's mayor and a deputy sheriff prevented any further discussion of the topic. However, the interruption brought Mike further problems. The mayor introduced himself but it was the deputy who immediately began to question Mike.

'I believe the paint outside is your horse.'

Mike nodded in agreement.

'That's strange. Never known the 4th to use paints and I served with them until I was wounded at the second battle of Bull Run.'

'You're quite right, deputy, it's my own and I own another one,' said Mike. He reached into the inside pocket of his tunic, produced the bill of sale for the paints and handed it to the mayor, who read it and then passed it to the deputy.

'That's fine,' said the deputy in a more friendly tone. 'No offence intended, Major, but with all the talk of Reb raids and escaped prisoners on the run, everything has to be checked out.'

'No offence taken, deputy,' replied Mike, silently noting that the deputy and not the sheriff called the shots. His suspicions were confirmed when the deputy left to conduct the late town patrol and the sheriff remained seated at the table.

But not for long.

'When he had the chance, Colonel O'Hallaran usually joined us in a game of friendly poker,' said the mayor. 'Do you play?'

'Just as long as it is friendly, a major's pay doesn't run to high stakes,' replied Mike cautiously.

But he needn't have worried, the sheriff proved to be an indifferent player and the mayor was even worse. However, he may have been distracted by the constant attentions of a very young and attractive saloon girl who served the drinks.

There was one other player.

'I've taken the liberty to ask Miss Marston to join us,' said the major. 'She will be leaving our little town soon and I thought she might like to give us the opportunity to win back some of the money she has already won from us.'

Her raven-coloured hair was neatly tied back by a deep red bow that exactly matched the colour of her gown and the little handbag she carried. And she soon proved she could play poker better than most men.

Her voice was softly sophisticated and suggested she had been brought up in New Hampshire or Maine, and yet Mike thought he occasionally detected a very slight Texas accent. She was extremely attractive, especially when she smiled. Her refined manner and exquisite dress taste immediately convinced Mike that whatever else she might be, she was not a saloon girl. So what was such an apparent lady doing in a saloon?

The card game was only a few minutes old when Mike found out. Miss Marston was an extremely talented poker player. A professional gambler no less! So it was no surprise when she amassed a large pile of winnings, even though the stakes were modest. Mike was also in front when, a little after midnight, the game broke up. The mayor finally succumbed to the advances of the very young saloon girl who had been his constant companion all evening. Indeed, since he had mentioned that his wife was away and would not be returning that night, she had been closer to him than a rash. Little wonder, thought Mike, that the mayor had lost the most money. Nevertheless, he was smiling broadly as he left.

The sheriff looked less happy about his losses. Nevertheless, he had another surprise for Mike.

'Stay here for the night, Major. There's plenty of spare rooms along the corridor but I think you will find number seven is the best. Of course, there will be no charge and I'll arrange for your paint to be stabled for the night before I turn in.'

'Thank you, Sheriff. Make a pleasant change to sleep in a bed.'

'Splendid. I'll make the necessary arrangements. So, if you will excuse me, Miss Marston, I'll take my leave.'

The sheriff left, closing the door behind him. That left Mike alone with Miss Marston, but it didn't seem to bother her at all.

Although Mike had not yet obtained any civilian clothes, the main purpose for his visit to the town, he was still pleased with the way the night had gone. He had added another twenty-five dollars to their pot and his impersonation of Major Hancock seemed to have fooled everybody. Well almost everybody.

'Room seven is the last room on the right,' said Miss Marston as she too began to collect her winnings and put them into the little red handbag. 'But I doubt you will be needing it.'

Startled, Mike looked up to see that Miss Marston had a little derringer pistol in her right hand and it was pointed directly at him.

'I know that you are not Major Hancock. So, suppose you drop this charade and tell me who you really are,' she said, her eyes glinting angrily. Mike noticed that under her northern façade her Texas drawl was now more distinct.

'You're mistaken,' was all he could think to say.

To Mike's surprise, she picked up a coin and threw it towards him. Without thinking, he caught it with his right hand.

'Hancock was left-handed and a terrible poker player. You are right-handed and almost as good a poker player as me. So are you Kyle?'

With a derringer pointed at his chest, there was little point in bluffing.

'No, we escaped together. Hancock was killed in the train wreck. I swapped uniforms. When the second train came I bluffed my way out with Kyle pretending to be my prisoner.'

'Did you search Hancock's body? He was carrying something that belonged to me.'

'Yes I did, but I found nothing apart from his wallet, some old documents and a key.'

'Show me all of it and be very careful to keep your hands in full view,' she ordered.

Mike did as he was bid. He was surprised when she showed no interest in the wallet or the documents but concentrated all her attention on the key. So much so he could have easily drawn his six-gun, but he wasn't about to shoot a woman no matter how desperate his position.

'I'll keep this,' she said still clutching the key in her left hand. 'You can keep the rest if you tell me where you are meeting up with Kyle.'

'There's absolutely nothing you can do to make me tell you that,' said Avison grimly.

'Oh, I think there is,' she said smiling beguilingly. 'I too have a plan to escape.'

Twenty minutes later and utterly bewildered, Mike found himself safely ensconced in room seven, certain that the secret of his deception was in safe hands.

He had listened in amazement, fascinated by the plan for their escape as it was outlined by the woman who had already proven to be so much more than she seemed to be.

Of course, in the time available she hadn't been able to fill in the details. That was what he was trying to do when he was interrupted by a knock at the bedroom door.

It wasn't Clara Marston, it was a saloon girl, but she was no longer in her saloon gown. Instead, she was wearing a loosely tied black robe; so loosely tied it was quite clear she was wearing nothing under it. She was carrying a bottle of whiskey and two glasses.

'Aren't you going to ask me in? A mutual friend suggested to me that you might like some company for the rest of the night.'

'Yes, of course,' he stammered.

That mutual friend could only have been Clara Marston. It appeared that the saloon girl was a part of her plan she had not divulged to Mike. He made a note to complain to her about it and then changed his mind. The saloon girl removed her robe and he had been right; she was wearing nothing under it.

Next morning he was rudely awakened as, six-gun in hand, the deputy sheriff burst into the bedroom. In spite of being naked, the saloon girl was quite unperturbed.

'What can I do for you, deputy? It's my day off so after Major Hancock has finished with me, I'm available,' she said cheekily.

The deputy blushed and then holstered his six-gun.

'Sorry to disturb you, Major, but your horse is missing and so is Miss Marston. I thought you might have gone together. We have reason to suspect that she might have been an agent for the South. The mayor's wife is expected to bring information to confirm it when she returns on this afternoon's stagecoach. Until then, I've been trying to keep Miss Marston in Clantonville without arousing her suspicions.'

'So why don't you go and catch her? The major and me have some unfinished business,' said the saloon girl, smiling wistfully at Mike.

'I'm about to. From letters she left we believe she's riding south. There's a posse waiting outside for me, but before I leave I'll see you get a decent replacement mount and saddle,' said the deputy before taking his leave.

Almost before the door had closed, the saloon girl climbed on top of Mike. In spite of their night of intimacy, her body still writhed with passion, so it was not surprising that it took her over an hour to complete her unfinished business with Mike.

CHAPTER SIX

ACROSS THE RIVER

'Saddle up, Lieutenant Kyle. No time to explain, we have
a long ride before we can met up with Mr Avison,' ordered
the female rider.

'How do you know my name and Avison's?' he asked.

'Answers later. There's bound to be a posse on my tail.
Believe it or not, I'm as much wanted by the Yankees as
you are.'

She had called Mike by his real name, not Major
Hancock. So, pausing only to collect the food he had 'lib-
erated' from the mayor's house and stuff it into his
saddle-bag, Jeff saddled up and mounted his skewbald
paint. After a few minutes' hard riding his new companion
signalled Jeff to slow down. After that they continued at
walking pace and she began to explain.

'I'm Clara Marston. Because I was brought up in the
North, the Yankees thought I was one of them, but I was
born in Texas and proud of it.'

'Born in Texas, I guess that's all I need to know,' said Jeff.

His ready acceptance of the situation won the most gorgeous smile from his new companion. Being dressed as a man made no difference; she was all woman. Jeff had never met her like and she must have noticed his admiration for she blushed profusely before hastily looking away.

They rode north-west, resting the horses only when absolutely necessary. Fear of pursuit occasioned that. At first, Clara led although she did not know her precise destination, her aim being simply to reach the river in which Jeff and Mike had made their escape. When they reached it, Jeff guessed they were roughly four days' ride north of the bridge.

'What now?' he asked Clara.

'Now we wait for your friend Mike, though how he's going to find us, I just don't know.'

'That's because you're not a scout,' laughed Jeff. 'I'll find a good place to camp and then we can wait for him to find us. He was a scout for Jeb Stuart after all.'

'He served under General Stuart! He never told me that,' exclaimed Clara.

'Oh he will, over and over again, you can bet on it,' laughed Jeff.

It was the first time Clara had seen Jeff smile. As he did, he seemed to shed years of worry and she warmed to the effect.

But only on the inside. Evening was approaching and the temperature was falling rapidly. Unused to the outdoor life, Clara began to shiver quite noticeably. Jeff dismounted, took off his grey tunic and offered it to his new companion.

'If you don't mind wearing a battle-worn and river-stained tunic, Miss Marston, it should help to keep the chill out.'

'Mind? I count it an honour to wear the uniform of someone who has fought for the Confederacy,' she replied huskily as she fought to restrain her emotions. In front of her was a man who, according to Mike, had repeatedly risked his life in the Shenandoah Valley for the Confederate cause.

As they continued, Jeff thought he detected tears in the corners of her eyes but at that moment he caught sight of a possible camping site. By the time he had examined and then rejected it she had recovered and they rode on in silence; he was occupied with looking for somewhere to camp, while she was lost in thoughts of what the future might bring.

Around Clara's neck was a plain gold necklace, a family heirloom. Attached to it but tucked out of sight under her shirt was the key she had taken at gunpoint from Mike when he was masquerading as Major Hancock. Before she met Jeff she had been sure that this key would not only unlock a strongbox but it would also open the way to a bright and prosperous future. But the strongbox was stored in the town of Independence. Unfortunately, that town was many days' ride away. Worse still, it was north-west of their present position and she was quite sure that Jeff and Mike would turn south towards the Confederate lines as soon as they were reunited.

It was almost dark before Jeff eventually located a suitable camping site, situated about a couple of hundred yards away from the river against whose current he had swum so valiantly. The campsite was nothing more than a shallow dell surrounded by a clump of trees. Altogether, it was not so dissimilar to the one he and Avison had camped on the first night of the escape. Mike had chosen that campsite. Therefore, Jeff hoped Mike would guess that he would choose a similar location.

In spite of the earlier storm, there were enough twigs and dry wood to light a fire without creating too much tell-tale smoke, so Jeff did not hesitate. While he lit the fire, his companion, with an ease that suggested her upbringing had been far removed from the life she had recently led, unsaddled the paints. By the time she had finished the fire was blazing merrily.

'How did you make the fire?' she said as she warmed herself.

'Practice, Miss Marston. It's a poor cavalry man that can't light a fire or travels without food,' he said as reached into his saddle-bag and passed her a chicken leg.

Although she had ridden often as a child, her more recent life in Washington had been far more genteel. So it was not surprising she was tired and stiff. After they had eaten, Jeff showed her how to use her saddle as a pillow. In spite of the hard ground, she was asleep in seconds.

Used to the rigours of war, he kept watch over her. He had no idea what the unpredictable Mike had in mind for the future but he had no doubt that he would soon find them. He was right, attracted by the firelight the former scout for Jeb Stuart arrived a little after midnight.

'You've done well, boy,' was his opening comment.

'Good to see you, too,' chuckled Jeff, who had come to like the big Texan and his bluff ways.

'Listen,' said Mike earnestly, 'I'll explain what happened later but for now I'm absolutely bushed. If I'm to be of any use tomorrow, I need sleep.'

'That's all right, old man. Guess you old-timers need to get your head down.'

Any other time, such a remark would have earned a stinging retort, but all through last night the saloon girl's sexual appetite had been insatiable. Since then there had been no time to rest and barely time for a hurried breakfast. After which, he had collected the replacement horse and saddle promised him by the deputy sheriff.

Mike had been pleasantly surprised to find that his new steed, a bay, was far better than the usual stable nag. Then he had ridden in the wrong direction in case he was being followed. Only when he was sure he had not been did he turn towards the river in which he and Jeff had swum to escape the Yankees. Then, he had ridden northwards along its bank before turning eastwards back towards Clantonville until he had reached the site where he and Jeff had set up their temporary camp.

As Mike had expected, the campsite was deserted. So, after he had rested his bay horse, he had set off again following the tracks left by Clara Marston and Jeff's horses. As a seasoned scout, he had no difficulty in following them until he saw their camp fire. After such a long ride and with little rest the night before he started, it was no wonder he fell asleep so quickly.

Jeff remained on guard for another hour before he too went to sleep, but he slept for only a few hours. A little before dawn he rebuilt the fire and waited for his companions to wake up. He didn't have to wait long; as soon as the sun began to rise, Mike began to stir.

'We need a new plan,' he said as he pulled on his boots. 'We can't keep riding northwards, that's Union territory and so is anywhere to the east. Yet if we turn round and head back south we're bound to run slap bang into anyone following us.'

'You figure they will send troops after us?' asked Jeff.

'By now they will have buried the dead from the train wreck, so they are bound to realize my story about a Reb ambush and escorting you to Washington was false. My guess is that they have already sent out patrols to find us. Hopefully, they assumed we turned south and sent most patrols in that direction. Unfortunately, Yankee patrols are not our main worry. Although the town's sheriff isn't too bright, his stiff-legged deputy is pretty smart. He and the mayor will work it out sooner rather than later and send a posse after us.'

'Why?' asked Jeff.

'It's not just us they will be after. The deputy hinted that he thought Miss Marston might be a Confederate spy. Leaving the way she did will only confirm his suspicions.'

'She said there might be a posse chasing her so we can't stay here much longer. Crossing the river and then heading west seems our best option,' said Jeff.

'But what about Miss Marston? She's an eastern-raised girl. There's no way she's going to be able to ride across that river.'

'Not on an empty stomach, for sure.' Clara Marston had been awake for some time, but had chosen to listen to the conversation. After all, she was alone in the wilds with two men she hardly knew.

Light rain began to fall. Used to life in the open, the men scarcely noticed it. But for a girl used to a nice bed and an indoor life, the conditions were far from ideal. While Jeff got a little more food out of his saddle-bags, Mike scouted the area to ensure there were no patrols nearby.

After breakfast, Clara Marston took charge.

'Mr Avison, or whatever your rank is, what makes you think this Texas-born girl can't ford a river?'

'It's the current. It's dangerously strong due to the storm after the twister. I know Jeff and me swam against the current to escape from the train crash but we are both expert swimmers. No disrespect Miss Marston; if you tried to swim across the river, in the unlikely event of you not drowning, the current would sweep you downstream, straight back to the enemy.'

'I wasn't thinking of swimming, Mr Avison. Got a rope?'

'Sure. In another life, I used to be a cowboy. Last thing I did before I left Clantonville was to buy one.'

'I don't see how a rope is going to help,' said Jeff.

'Most Texans, especially cowboys, call a lasso a rope,' explained Mike, grinning at Jeff's ignorance.

'So how is a rope as you call it going to help, Miss Marston?' asked Jeff.

'Put the rope, the lasso part, around my waist and then tie the rope around the pommel of the saddle of my horse; the rope will prevent me from being swept away and you can catch me if I get dragged under.'

'If you're sure,' said Mike doubtfully.

62

'Mr Avison, when I was just a little girl, I crossed the Red River roped to my pony. I was going east to stay with my aunt in order to get an eastern education. Afterwards, my pa was bushwhacked by rustlers and my uncle took over the ranch. So I stayed east but I never forgot I was born a Texan.'

They broke camp but made no attempt to disguise it from their pursuers. Indeed, Mike hoped their pursuers would find it and would then assume they had carried on north and not swam across the river. So while Jeff busied himself with the crossing arrangements, Mike laid some false tracks north; something he had done many times when riding for Jeb Stuart.

Although it was very hard and incredibly tiring even for their steeds, the crossing went without a hitch. However, there was no time for rest; they had to get out of sight of the river bank. Unfortunately, the ground on the opposite side of the river, as Mike had previously predicted, was flat and featureless, affording no cover whatsoever. Yet the two paints and the bay were exhausted after their hard swim.

Jeff made the decision. If they were seen, they would need their mounts to be as fresh as possible, so dripping wet and very cold in the fresh morning breeze, they walked the horses westwards directly away from the river.

The rain returned, not that it mattered since they were all soaking from their river ordeal. Looking straight ahead and shivering with cold, Clara trudged silently beside Mike's piebald paint. His eyes were never still as he constantly searched the plain for any Yankee patrols on this side of the river. However, there was not the slightest sign of life. In the meantime, Jeff kept watch behind them, focusing on the other side of the river, but like the plains in front of them, the river banks also remained deserted.

After an hour, they remounted their steeds and rode slowly westwards, not knowing what was in front of them. The plain, however, seemed endless, as did the rain. However, by mid-afternoon the following day both had begun to come to an end. Indeed, after less than another hour, they came across a small group of buildings. The largest was a cabin and next to it was a small outhouse. Sandwiched between it and the smallest barn Mike had even seen was a small corral.

Whether the cabin was a line shack denoting the boundary of some huge ranch or whether it was a failed homestead, they neither knew nor cared. Apart from some hens, it was deserted. As both horses and riders were still soaking wet and near exhaustion the homestead or whatever else it was offered a dry sanctuary.

While Jeff unsaddled the horses, Mike checked out the cabin. Inside, there were three rooms. The main one was sparsely furnished with only a crudely fashioned table and four basic chairs. There was also an oil lamp and a small cupboard that had evidently been used to store food. Unfortunately, apart from a small quantity of flour, it was empty. The second, much smaller, room contained a dresser, one chair and a bed. The third, even smaller room was just large enough to contain a single bed. Under the bed was and a small holdall, or carpetbag as they were better known in Texas. The dustiness of the cabin convinced him that it had not been used for some time, so he did not bother to open the carpetbag. Instead, he went outside to examine the outbuildings.

64

The small barn was empty but in the outhouse he found a large amount of kindling and a huge pile of logs. They had obviously been there for some time. In spite of the rain and the recent storms, they were all bone dry.

Since the need to dry out their clothes was great, Mike decided to risk lighting a fire. By the time Jeff had finished tending to the horses and brought in the saddle-bags, Clara Marston was warming herself in front of it. Her sopping wet clothes were actually steaming.

'What on earth have you got in your saddle-bags, Miss Marston? They weigh twice as much as ours put together!'

'Lieutenant Kyle, a girl like me must have nice clothes to impress with. Besides, how far do you think you're going to get in that Reb uniform?' she retorted.

As she emptied her saddle-bags, Mike noted she had a couple of men's shirts among her blouses and skirts. As all her clothes had been thoroughly soaked during the river crossing and were still wet through, she laid them by the fire to dry and then went in search of towels with which to dry herself.

The rain having stopped, Mike decided to scout the surrounding countryside. While he did so, Jeff emptied the contents of his saddle-bags on to the table and sorted out the last of the food. Although it was very soggy, it was just about eatable but there was only enough for one more meal.

He was just thinking how Miss Marston would cope without regular meals when she came back into the room. Apart from a small towel wrapped round her head she was wearing only one other, so small that it barely covered her otherwise naked body.

At the same moment Mike re-entered the cabin.

'Oops,' he said, 'I didn't know you two had gotten so well acquainted.'

'No, it's nothing like that,' protested Jeff as his face turned beetroot red in embarrassment. 'Miss Marston. . . .'

'Miss Marston can speak for herself. If we are going to escape, we have to live together. I have to know I can trust you.'

'You can, within reason, Miss Marston. I can't speak for Jeff but there's a limit to how much this red-blooded old Texan can take no matter how honourable his intentions may have been.'

Jeff, too embarrassed to speak, could only nod his head in agreement.

'Then you two had better go outside while I get dressed,' she said chuckling at Jeff's obvious embarrassment and Mike's down to earth frankness. 'And when you come back in, my name's Clara.'

'Mine's Jeff,' replied Jeff. Mike, however, said nothing as they hurried out of the cabin.

They didn't have to wait outside for long. After only a few minutes, Clara called them back into the cabin. She was wearing a man's shirt, slacks and riding boots. Gone was all trace of make-up and her hair seemed much lighter. Yet, as before, there was no disguising her femininity even though she looked nothing like her former self. Jeff thought the changes made her look even more attractive.

Then, the horses outside began to neigh. Horses are naturally gregarious by nature and they were calling a welcome to one or more of their own. Had the posse from Clantonville caught up with them or was it a Yankee patrol?

CHAPTER SEVEN

POLLYANNA

'Clara, go into one of the bedrooms and stay there, no matter what happens,' ordered Mike.

Before she could argue he raced outside, determined to saddle at least one of the paints before the riders, whoever they were, arrived.

'Jeff, I can look after myself,' she said angrily.

'You may have to if it's the Clantonville posse or a Yankee patrol. Now, do as you're told. We're going to try to lead them away.'

He too was gone before she could reply. What sort of men were these who would put their lives in great danger for her, a virtual stranger, yet ask for nothing in return? She had no answer. Instead, she did as she had been instructed and went into one of the bedrooms, but not before she got her derringer out of her saddle-bag.

Outside, Jeff almost ran into Mike.

'Easy boy, we won't be running today, look yonder.

Jeff did as he was bid. Still some distance away was a small wagon pulled by just one horse. Amazingly it was another paint. Judging by the way it was struggling and the slow progress of the wagon, it was a saddle horse more used to being ridden than hauling a load.

As it drew nearer they could see the wagon was being driven by a woman. Her head was covered by a large shawl and she seemed to be encouraging the struggling paint by kindness rather than using her whip. But then, thought Jeff, paints were far more valuable than the more mundanely coloured but otherwise excellent mustangs.

As she drew nearer, Mike could tell she was quite young in spite of the shawl that almost covered her. As she saw them her alarm was plain to see. Yet she continued to drive straight towards the little cabin.

'Who are you and what are you doing in my home?' the woman demanded as she dismounted. She held a Springfield musket but it was not aimed at them. It seemed she had no fear of them even though she was alone.

'We're just travellers who took shelter from the rain,' replied Mike.

'Travellers! I think not. The whole Territory knows there's a dangerous Confederate officer on the run. So how come you haven't taken him prisoner, Major?' she asked as she saw Jeff standing in her doorway. Of course, he was still wearing his grey officer's uniform.

'I mean you no harm,' said Jeff sincerely.

'Nor I, ma'am,' said Mike. 'But it's a long story we have to tell.'

'I'm sure it is, Major, I look forward to hearing it, so

shall we move inside?'

'First, I'll tend to your horse, ma'am. Your mare needs a good rub down. She doesn't look right hauling a wagon,' said Jeff.

'You're right, Lieutenant, unfortunately I have no other option.'

'It looks as if we're not the only ones with a story to tell,' said Clara. She had heard a female voice and, her curiosity aroused, decided to leave the security of the bedroom and join them.

If the woman was surprised to see Clara dressed in men's clothing, she did not show it. On the contrary, when she took off her shawl it was Mike who was surprised. About thirty, sun-tanned and quite tall, she had corn-coloured hair, hazel eyes and a taut willowy figure that suggested she was no stranger to hard work. Not only Clara noticed that the suntan was broken on the third finger of her left hand suggesting that she had until recently she had been married.

'When you've all stopped inspecting me, perhaps you'd all care to introduce yourselves,' the woman snapped defiantly.

When angered her Southern drawl was quite unmistakable.

Mike made the introductions, although he called himself Major Hancock.

'I'm Pollyanna Cooper. I was married until my fool of a husband got himself drowned trying to cross that damned river.'

'Sorry to hear that, ma'am. Was he in the Army?'

'Not likely,' she snorted. 'Nearest he got to soldiering

was across the card table. He always figured that young officers were easy prey until they caught him cheating. Then, there was that dreadful twister. During the confusion it caused he escaped by stealing a horse.

'They raised a posse and chased him to the river. In spite of the storm my fool husband tried to cross the river to get back here. He didn't make it. They found his body near the railway bridge. He never had a lick of common sense.'

'I sorry to hear about your loss, but even if he had made it across the river, wouldn't the posse have followed as soon as the level had returned to normal?' asked Clara.

'Or they could have ridden downstream and crossed by the railroad bridge.' said Mike thoughtfully.

'They might, but as long as I had time to hide his horse, they wouldn't have known he was here,' Pollyanna said mysteriously.

'Well, if we may trespass on your hospitality a little longer, we will be on our way after dark, tonight,' said Mike, changing the subject.

'And how far do you think you will get dressed like that, Johnny Reb?' Pollyanna laughed scornfully as she pointed to Jeff's Confederate uniform.

'Mrs Cooper, what else can we do?' asked Clara.

'Well, you can stop calling me Mrs Cooper for a start. Pollyanna will do just fine. You will be safe here for tonight and tomorrow at least. Then, if you've still a mind to leave, perhaps under cover of darkness tomorrow night would be as good a time as any.'

'Thank you,' said Clara. 'I'm not used to roughing it and crossing the river has taken its toll on me, and our horses are almost done for.'

'Well, that's settled then,' said Mike, smiling gratefully at Pollyanna.

Clara noticed that as Pollyanna returned his smile her face seemed to soften, making her look years younger. However, it was Jeff to whom she spoke.

'Lieutenant, if you would go to my wagon you will find coffee in the back, and while you're at it put your saddles in the barn and cover them with straw. Then put your paints in the corral with mine. If anybody comes, I might be able to explain away the paints, but not your Army saddles.'

Hot coffee and cold chicken; Jeff Kyle had known far worse. But what next? He was the real officer so the escape plan should be down to him. Unfortunately, the added complication of Clara – even in men's clothes he found her disturbingly attractive – clouded his thought processes to such an extent that he was unable to think clearly. Hopefully a good sleep would clear his mind.

It didn't. The men slept in the barn taking turns to keep guard while the women slept soundly in the cabin. Guard duty gave Jeff ample time to think about what to do next; to ride south meant they would almost certainly run into cavalry troops or the Clantonville posse if they had crossed the river by the railroad bridge. Riding north was to head further into Yankee territory, while westwards would eventually lead them into the Oklahoma Badlands, otherwise known as the Indian Territory.

Apart from a few well-fortified settlements, the Indian Territory was a vast untamed area, the home of several nomadic hostile Comanche tribes. The only thing Jeff knew about them was their fearsome reputation; it had often been said they were to be avoided if you wanted to stay alive.

He had, however, heard of a route through the Indian Territory. From here they would have to ride south-west for many days until they reached the Arkansas River. Having crossed it they would then also have to cross the oddly named North Canadian River. Even then, they would not be done with river crossings for the Washita, which flowed into the mighty Red River, still stood between them and Texas.

Dangerous in the extreme, this would have been their best route to safety, except that according to Mike all these rivers were subject to deadly flash floods and even in normal times some of them were wider than the one they had just crossed. He doubted if Clara, however plucky she undoubtedly was, would be able to cope with the long journey near enough a thousand miles, even more if they had to make detours to find suitable river crossings. Whatever, if anything, she thought of him, he was not about to desert her.

As dawn broke, he and Mike began grooming the horses, Jeff outlined his plan but Mike shook his head ruefully.

'Jeff, it's not known as the Indian Territory without good reason. Before we reach the Arkansas River we will be likely to encounter the Shawnee and believe me, few live to tell that tale.'

'But not if we travelled only at night and hid during the day, Indians don't attack at night, or so I've been told.'

'Don't believe that old wives' tales. Apart from being

hunters, the Shawnee are horse breeders and prize paints above all, as do most Prairie Indians. Shawnees won't let an old superstition stop them.'

'What superstition?' asked Jeff.

'If a brave is killed at night his spirit won't be able to find its way to the Indian version of heaven. It's white man's nonsense. When we cross their territory, nothing will stop the Shawnee trying to get our paints. Apart from riding them they could trade them to the Sioux. The last I heard, the rate is about one paint for four or even five mustangs. Unfortunately for us, no matter what tribe, a Plains Indian's wealth is calculated by the number of mustangs he owns.'

'You're right,' agreed Jeff. 'I heard that the more mustangs a brave possesses the more wives he is likely to get.'

'That's the way of the Comanche and the other Plains Indians as far as I know,' said Mike.

'You mean apart from the Sioux, Shawnee and Comanche, we are likely to encounter other Indian tribes?' asked Jeff.

'Too right. In my youth long before I joined up with Jeb Stuart's Cavalry, I was a cowboy. Then I became an Indian scout and spent many years deep in the Indian Territory. Some folks don't realize that part of it runs into north-west Texas.'

'Are these other Indian tribes as hostile as the Comanches?' asked Jeff, extremely impressed by his companion's knowledge of the Indian Territory.

'Some are. So even if we managed to cross the Arkansas River safely we would then be in Cherokee territory. In the unlikely event of riding across their domain undetected and then managing to cross the North Canadian River we would still be in great danger. To the west of the Washita River roam the Choctaw and to the south-east of the Choctaw live the Chickasaw. If that's not bad enough, the north-west is the realm of the Seminole Indians and some say they are the most hostile of all!'

'Then I guess you're right,' conceded Jeff. 'Even without Clara, the journey would be too dangerous.'

Unfortunately, Jeff could not come up with any other option that had any chance of success. Yet a possible solution to their problem came over breakfast and from a most unexpected source. They sat around the table while Pollyanna cooked breakfast. A heated debate broke between the three fugitives, so heated they forget their host was in the same room. The men were adamant that Clara could not survive the trek through the Indian Badlands to reach Texas. Therefore, they must turn back on their tracks and head eastwards crossing the river by the railroad bridge. However, Clara flatly refused to consider the idea.

'You can't turn back. The Yankees will have patrols looking out for you. If they catch you they will hang you both for sure. If I'm caught, the worst that can happen is that they will put me in jail for a few years.'

'Not true,' replied Mike. 'They think you're a spy, so you face a firing squad if you're caught.'

'That was always the chance I took. You must go on without me,' she said defiantly.

'Not a chance,' said Mike. 'I can't speak for Jeff, but. . . .'

'We go together or not at all,' interrupted the young

74

lieutenant, so fiercely that Clara turned abruptly and looked at him intently. For a second their eyes met. Then, equally abruptly, she turned away. Strange feelings began to envelop her as wildly improbable thoughts came unbidden into her mind. They were driven away by Mike as he reviewed their position.

'Although half of them belong to our young lieutenant, I've amassed quite a few dollars since we escaped. Enough to buy a change of clothes and then head eastwards until we can catch a train to St Louis. If we then run short of money we can take jobs until we have the fares to take a river boat along the Mississippi to New Orleans. Then, it shouldn't be too difficult to find a ship that's sailing around the coast to Galveston,' concluded Mike thoughtfully.

'No! I won't let you do it. Even if you had the right civilian clothes it would still be too dangerous,' Clara said, shaking herself out of the strange reverie that had temporarily overcome her.

'Well, we can't stay here,' said Jeff. 'Even if they cross the river by the railroad bridge, the posse will eventually arrive. No telling what they might do to Pollyanna if they find us here,' said Jeff.

'They won't find any of us here if you will let me help,' said Pollyanna as she brought the breakfast to the table.

'Why would you want to help us?' asked Mike.

'Because I want you to take me with you,' came the surprising response. 'I've been staying in town for a few weeks trying to raise some money until the bank manager convinced me that I can't make a go of this place on my own.'

'Pollyanna, speaking only for myself, I'd love to have

you along,' said Mike. 'But we barely have enough money for the three of us to get to Galveston.'

'As to that, I agree with Miss Clara,' replied Pollyanna, 'from what you have said, I think you're bound to be caught if you take that route. Besides I have a wagon.'

'It's only a small wagon. In any case, alone in the Badlands we wouldn't stand a chance against the Indian tribes,' protested Mike.

'Who said anything about crossing the Badlands?' Pollyanna replied.

'But what other way is there?' asked Clara.

'Unless you promise to take me with you, you will never know,' Pollyanna replied. 'I know you think I'm just a wife of a failed homesteader, but I've got an idea. I just need to think it through before I share it with you. Then, if you agree to it, all I ask in return is that you take me with you. Once we reach your destination, I'll look out for myself.'

'That seems fair enough,' agreed Mike. 'If you can come up with a better plan than ours before we leave tonight, you have our word you can come with us.'

Clara and Jeff nodded in agreement, although neither of them believed that Pollyanna was capable of devising any plan that would lead them to safety.

CHAPTER EIGHT

A NEW PLAN

They were quite wrong to doubt Pollyanna; a little after midday she summoned them to hear her plan.

'There is an old trail we might use to get to Texas,' she said, instantly attracting their attention.

'An old trail?' said Mike incredulously.

'Yes. But first we must travel even further north to a town called Independence.'

The key attached to the bottom links of Clara's gold necklace and therefore hidden under her shirt seemed to pulsate as she sharply caught her breath as she heard that town named. In the vault of the town bank was a trunk that only her key could unlock. She was not sure what it contained but her instructions had been clear; if the war was lost any documents inside must be destroyed. Whatever else was in the trunk would be hers to keep.

Fortunately, the attention of her two companions was completely focused on Pollyanna, so they failed to notice her shocked surprise and that gave time for Clara to recover her composure.

'What's important enough in Independence to make us travel even deeper into Union territory?' asked Jeff.

'Two old trails start from there; back in the old days before the War, the Oregon Trail was used by prospectors and their families during the California gold rush, but I guess it's the other one we want.'

'What other one?' asked Clara.

'The Santa Fe Trail, of course,' replied Pollyanna, surprised that Clara had not heard of it.

But then nor had Jeff. Seeing the blank looks on their faces, Mike explained.

'The Santa Fe Trail runs south-west across the Badlands, for most of the first 350 miles or so it travels through Osage territory.'

'Osage Indians? I haven't heard of that tribe,' said Jeff.

'Once hostile, they are said to be friendly to Palefaces, as they call us. Their true enemies are the Kiowa and most of the sub-tribes of the Comanche.'

'The Yankees won't expect us to travel north,' mused Jeff.

Clara thought long and hard. When they thought the homestead was in danger of being attacked by a Union patrol they had been prepared to risk their lives for her, a virtual stranger. Surely that was enough to earn her trust, even if she couldn't reveal all of her secret.

'Nor will the Clantonville posse, and even if I have to go alone it is my sworn duty to go to Independence.'

Jeff was about to ask why but was interrupted before he could do so.

'So, when do we start?' asked Pollyanna eagerly.

'We don't,' replied Mike. Seeing the look of immense disappointment on both Pollyanna's and Clara's faces, he began to explain. 'Pollyanna's wagon is built for light hauling, not traversing the Santa Fe Trail laden with enough provisions and water to last for up to six months. And, just as important, our paints are saddle horses. So even if we could buy a prairie wagon, and I guess the Yankee Army has already requisitioned most of them from round here, we would still need the right sort of horses to pull it and they don't come cheap.'

'Major Hancock, have you any other objections to my plan?' asked Pollyanna.

'No,' he replied.

'I thought you might raise objections. So let me ask you, how can you hope to escape detection riding such beautiful horses? Apart from my own Joey, I doubt that there is another paint within two hundred miles of here.'

'Splendid animals, but they are a problem for sure,' admitted Mike ruefully. 'Unfortunately, selling or trading them is too risky. Although I have bills of ownership for them, they're in the name of Major Hancock and I guess every Yankee patrol from here to St Louis is on the lookout for me by now.'

'I won't ask you why,' said Pollyanna. 'Nevertheless, I could sell your horses or even exchange them without anybody being any the wiser.'

'How so, ma'am?' asked Mike.

'If you don't stop calling me ma'am, Major Hancock, I swear I will turn you in myself.'

'Sorry, Pollyanna,' he replied sheepishly.

'That's better. Now, as you know, I too have a paint and I've had several offers for her, so providing you have a legitimate bill of sales for your two I'm sure that Mr Drury, the owner of the stables in Smithville, will buy all three without asking too many awkward questions. Of course, we won't get the full value for them but it should be enough to get a couple of more suitable horses, and perhaps I could trade in my own little wagon for something more substantial.'

'It's a good plan but with all the provisions, ammunition and water; you and Clara, plus either Jeff or me, it would need at least four stout horses or half a dozen stout mules to pull a prairie schooner along the Santa Fe Trail,' said Mike.

'Provided we go to Independence you can use my poker winnings, they should be more than enough to buy the extra horses,' said Clara.

So Pollyanna's plan was agreed, except that one of the men would accompany her to Smithville to help choose horses suitable for pulling a large wagon. As her late husband's clothes fitted Mike reasonably well it was natural that the role fell to him. Pollyanna was delighted for she had already begun to formulate another scheme, although this one was of a far more personal nature. However, for the time being she remained silent on the matter. Nevertheless, she had another surprise in store for them.

'Jeff, while we're away, you might like to move the bed in the small bedroom. If you then pull back the rug you will find a trapdoor leading to an underground chamber.

My late husband stored several crates of weapons. I don't know much about guns but he did tell me that some of the rifles packed in the crates were worth a lot of money.'

Early next morning, they started out. Pollyanna drove the cart with the Springfield musket primed and loaded at her feet. Not that she intended to use it but Major Hancock insisted she kept it near her. Although dressed in civilian clothes, Mike intended to keep up the pretence of being a Yankee officer, at least until they had completed their mission. That way his new companion could not inadvertently give away his true identity.

The cart was again pulled by Pollyanna's paint, which as Mike had surmised was normally a saddle horse. To ease the paint's discomfort, he rode the bay loaned to him by Clantonville's deputy sheriff, although the chances of that horse ever being returned to him looked pretty remote. Although Mike kept close by the cart, his eyes were never still as he searched for any sign of Yankee patrols or pursuit from the Clantonville posse.

During a rest period for the horses, Pollyanna began to put her second, highly personal plan into action.

'Major Hancock, I hope you won't object, but to make this work, you will have to pretend to be my man so when we get to Smithville I shall not object to you putting your arm around my waist or holding hands and you had better start calling me Polly.'

Mike was so taken aback he could no longer continue his masquerade.

'I should be honoured to call you Polly, but I'm not a major nor even a Yankee officer. My real name is Mike Avison and I'm a Reb scout, rank of sergeant, or at least I was until I got taken prisoner.'

'So how come you were wearing a Yankee uniform when we met?'

Avison began by recounting some of his adventures while serving under the maverick Confederate commander General Jeb Stuart and then finished by relating his life since the train wreck, only omitting his recent night of passion.

Polly listened in rapt attention and then was silent for a while. Blushing deeply, she plucked up enough courage to take their pretend relationship a step further.

'Mike, if we are to convince Mr Drury we are really together we shall have to act, in public at least, like . . .' she hesitated, acutely embarrassed.

'Like what?' asked Mike gently.

'Like lovers,' she barely whispered the words.

At noon they reached Smithsville. Although it was little more than a settlement, it had a large livery stable. Its owner, Jack Drury, had for months tried to buy Polly's paint; now, although he did not yet know it, he would have the chance to buy three!

Unfortunately, when they eventually arrived Drury wasn't there. Apart from running the stables he was the nearest thing Smithsville had to a vet and he was also a part-time deputy. He had ridden out to another homestead to tend to a sick mare and was not expected back until much later that afternoon. Mike used some of the time to look out for a heavy wagon or even a prairie schooner but failed to find anything suitable. It seemed the Yankee soldiers had indeed commandeered all of them.

While they were still waiting, they had a meal in the settlement's only hotel, a small affair with just a few rooms. The meal was plain but well cooked.

'We're not going to finish our business today,' said Polly. 'I think we will have to stay the night.'

'You're right. I'll book us two rooms and then take the horses to the stables.'

He made to get up but Polly shook her head and stopped him.

'No Mike. Remember what I said on the trail. You're supposed to be my new man and the one I'm going to be uprooting my life for. How's it going to look if we have separate rooms?'

'You're right. While I book us in, perhaps you will see if Drury has returned?'

Mike booked the room and ordered a bath for later, then he made his way over to the livery stables with the horses. It seemed that Drury had indeed returned and was engaged in an animated conversation with Polly.

'Hello, darling,' she said to a surprised Mike. He was even more surprised when she slipped her arm round his waist and kissed him. Surprised until he remembered she was only play-acting the part of his girl. Unbidden, a pang of disappointment ran through him.

'Darling, Mr Drury has offered us a deal, but I know so little about horses can you help?'

The way she smiled and unashamedly fluttered her eyebrows at Mike it almost took his breath away. But it was Mr Drury who took centre stage.

'Major Hancock, how come you're not in uniform?'

'Because I'm a scout. I've a few days leave left before I

have to go back north, so I'm using them to get my personal life together. The Civil War can't last forever.'

'Major, I won't deny that. You know, I've been trying to buy your good lady's paint for months, now I find you've two more for sale. Do you have bills of sale for them?'

'Yes, I do.'

'Fine, then I can offer you a very good deal. For your three paints and the cart, I know where I can get hold of an almost new prairie wagon the Union Army missed when they commandeered all the settlement's wagons, and a fine pair of dray horses to pull it. But my official duties will keep me here for the rest of the day so I can't get them until tomorrow.'

'We can wait, but what are dray horses?' asked Polly.'

'European horses specifically bred to pull a flat cart designed to carry heavy or bulky loads,' said Mr Drury.

The puzzled expression on Polly's face showed that she was no wiser, so Mike intervened.

'By flat carts, I think Mr Drury means ones that have no sides. They are usually called drays.'

They made their way back to the hotel and ate dinner, by which time the bath had been drawn. Polly went first and after luxuriating for about half an hour returned to their bedroom covered only by a large towel. Under the towel she had a surprisingly curvaceous figure. Not wishing to take advantage of the situation nor trusting his feelings, for he found Polly disturbingly attractive, Mike left the bedroom immediately. To his surprise he found the bathtub had been topped up with what must have been near boiling water. So he too soaked himself. But, conscious of Polly's presence, he was fully dressed when he returned to the bedroom.

Not so Polly, she had got into bed and *all* her clothes were neatly piled upon a nearby chair. Mike sat down on the other chair and made to go to sleep but he was immediately interrupted by Polly.

'Do you not want to come to bed?' she asked plaintively.

'Yes. But no man could lie beside you without . . .' his voice tailed off in embarrassment.

'Mike Avison, step by step the decisions I've made have brought us to this point even if I hadn't deliberately intended then to do so. It was me that suggested we should act like lovers. So, I can hardly blame you if you take advantage of the situation. Even if I wanted to object I couldn't without giving our cover away and I'm so desperate to get away from here, you know I wouldn't do that.'

Mike looked long at the outline of Polly's naked body tantalisingly covered by just a single cotton sheet. Of course he wanted her, but not like this.

'Pollyanna, I have slept with enough saloon girls to understand just one thing about women.'

'And what is that, Mike?' she said sharply.

'That casual sex is best with saloon girls. You and I would make poor bedfellows. I fear that you might dislike yourself and me in the morning.'

'And if I said I would take the risk?'

'In what now seems a different life I was once happily married. Since my wife died I've been a fighting man. Of course, I have bedded a few saloon girls but I've never ever thought of settling down again with another woman and living a normal life until I met you. But I guess it's much too soon to start hoping there's any chance you might. . . .'

Polly smiled beguilingly and very slowly began to pull back the bed sheet. When she was half uncovered, she tantalisingly stopped.

'Too soon, Mike? Not so. Why do you think I insisted on leaving my homestead and going with you to Texas?'

With that, she kicked away the blanket, revealing the full nakedness of her slim and lithe body, hardened by the toil of running a homestead. In Mike's eyes Polly was far more erotically alluring than any painted saloon girl.

'Mike, my husband was not a sensible man. Always, there was another scheme to get rich quickly but none of them ever worked and we finished up at the homestead near to where I was born. Even then he spent far more time planning new get-rich-quick schemes or gambling than he did working on the homestead.'

'Then it must have been hard for you to make ends meet,' said Mike.

'What made it harder was I lost all respect for him. The only thing I can say in his favour was he never chased after other women. So now I'm not proud to be so wantonly forward, acting no better than the saloon girls you say you've bedded. But then, you could be gone tomorrow, so I haven't the time to be more ladylike. If after tonight you don't want me again, so be it.'

In spite of his best intentions Mike Avison could not resist such temptation. They made love all night, but it wasn't just sex. Indeed, he had known from the start it would be far more. As dawn broke, passion spent, he pulled her into his arms and, bodies intertwined, they fell asleep. When they awoke he kissed her gently and then proved her fears he would not want her again were completely groundless. Indeed, it was she that broke off their love making; breakfast called and they had a busy morning ahead.

CHAPTER NINE

THE SHIRE-HORSES

As they made their way to the stables, doubts began to cloud Polly's mind. Last night and earlier this morning she had shamelessly thrown herself at Mike. Then he had been both caring and reassuring. But with passion spent, how did he now feel? Did he still want her? His arm wrapped reassuringly around her waist was all the answer she needed.

Oddly, there was no sign of the paints but Mike's borrowed mount was still in the stable. Drury's stable lad explained that his boss had left at dawn and had taken the paints to the home of a wealthy stud rancher who not only had two daughters but also had a second wife considerably younger than himself. For that reason Mr Drury had said he was confident he would be able to sell all the paints at a very good price However, the lad also said his boss was not expected to return until much later that day.

They whiled away the time slowly walking arm-in-arm round the settlement and exchanging pleasantries with the folk they met. They had enjoyed a hearty breakfast and neither he nor Polly were really hungry but Mike had spent too many days in the Reb army without food to miss the chance of a cooked meal. So he insisted they had a large cooked lunch in the settlement's only restaurant.

Over lunch, Mike suddenly became very serious.

'About last night,' he began and then paused as if he was struggling to say what was on his mind.

Suddenly Polly's fears began to resurface; was he about to say something like although the sex had been good he was not ready to settle down yet? Had he changed his mind about taking her with him when they left the homestead?

He had not. In fact it soon became clear he had quite the opposite on his mind, but not before he had given her quite a fright.

'I've only a little money. The clothes on my back were your ex-husband's. Yankee patrols are looking out for me and when this war is over I'll be starting from scratch.'

'So what are you saying?' She dared not look him in the eye for fear she would see rejection in them.

'After the hardship you've endured that's not the life you deserve.'

'Do I get any say in the matter?'

'Always. In this case your word is final.'

'Mike, I don't understand what you're trying to say.'

'I've been around long enough to know the real thing – after all I had it with Becky. I didn't think I'd find it again but like I say I think you deserve a better life than I can offer you.'

'Becky was your wife?'

'Yes, she was just sixteen when we married. Back then I was just a dollar a day cowboy. That wasn't really enough for two to live on so when I was offered the job of civilian scout for the US Cavalry I jumped at it. Although the pay wasn't that much more, the Army provided free accommodation, and Becky loved Army life.'

'What happened?'

'The Civil War. By then I had been promoted to lance corporal but my unit had almost as many Confederate sympathizers as Union men, so we were disbanded. The South desperately needed scouts and I was offered the position of corporal. Becky begged me not to join up but I did anyway. I left her and our baby with some good friends in Virginia. I never saw alive her again. Our friends were abolitionists, even though they supported the South. Vigilantes burnt down their house; Becky and my little girl died in the fire. They caught the perpetrators and hanged them. That was almost four years ago.'

'I'm so sorry for your loss, Mike. Unlike you I was more relieved than grieved when my husband drowned. But to come back to the present, you just said that my word is final. But final about what?'

'Us. Whether we have a future together.'

'Yes, Mike we do; for as long as you want me I'm your woman.'

'You're that sure even though you hardly know me?'

'Yes. Anyway, after last night we are not exactly strangers,' she replied blushing deeply.

They had barely finished lunch when Drury returned

driving a prairie schooner pulled by two huge and magnificent horses the like of which Mike Avison had never
before seen. In spite of their huge size they were magnifi-
cently proportioned; both had deep and wide chests,
suggesting they were as strong as they looked. Both were
jet black in colour except for their lower legs, which were
white and had long fine hair, known as feathers, flowing
from them. They were virtually identical and clearly twins.

'Afternoon, Major,' called Drury. 'Ain't these two beau-
ties. They're English horses some call Shires. They're
yours if we can come to an understanding. I've left your
paints at the stud ranch with the rancher's wife and his
girls. That's a horse dealer's trick that never fails. I'll go
back in a day or so and they will have persuaded old man
Grey to buy them. I'm so confident of selling them I'll cut
you a good deal now.'

He didn't add that by buying the paints today and
selling them in a few days' time he expected to make a
handsome profit. Instead, he climbed down from the
prairie schooner, leaving the reins free, before speaking to
Pollyanna.

'Don't be afraid of their size. Believe me, they are the
most amiable beasts you will ever find.'

Seeing that she was somewhat daunted by their size,
Drury continued his sales pitch.

'Climb up and grab the reins, then take them for a spin.
Just say "walk on" when you want to start, "trot now", when
you want to go a little faster and then, "whoa", when you
want to stop. You will find they are very obedient.'

She did as she was bid and after a few minutes drove out
of the yard.

'Don't worry, Major Hancock, the Shires won't bolt. They're placid by nature and too big to be scared by anything. Now while Pollyanna is away what say we grab a cup of coffee in my office? We've business to discuss and its best done in private.'

In silence they walked to Drury's office.

'Pour yourself a cup of coffee and grab a chair while I lock the door. Best if we're not disturbed.'

Feeling ill at ease, Mike did as he was bid.

'Smithsville is too small to have a full-time law officer. Don't pay much but I act as part-time deputy. In that capacity I received a message asking me to keep a look out for two riders on paints and here you are, with two to sell, plus Pollyanna's.'

Mike began to reach for his gun.

'No need for that,' said Drury hastily. 'Hear me out first.'

'Go on, but make it good.'

'The war is almost over, Major. For those in the know there's a very strong rumour that the South is soon to surrender. So there's no profit in turning you in, especially as the Union will claim back your paints. As I've already said, together with Pollyanna's they're as good as sold.'

'So, what do you propose?' asked Mike.

'I am a man of my word. I intend to complete the deal as promised. Just so long as you leave immediately and give me your word that you will only return once.'

'Only once, I don't understand?'

'There's only one trail from Pollyanna's homestead suitable for a heavily loaded wagon and it leads right here to Smithsville. On your return, be my guest. Stay a couple of nights at the hotel. I'll foot the bill as part of the deal. Might be a long time before you sleep in a proper bed again. But then, when you leave, don't look back and don't ever return. Your word on it or I'll have to turn you in.'

'You think you could outdraw me?' asked Mike ominously.

'Maybe not, Major. But I think you're a decent enough man not to take an unfair advantage. Then there's Pollyanna. You wouldn't want her to spend the rest of her life on the run with you, would you?'

'No. Once we've completed the deal, we will drive back to Pollyanna's spread to pack her belongings and then return here. I'll take up your offer to stay in the hotel and then leave Smithville for good. You have my word.'

'Fair enough. Now as to the deal, the Shires must be worth at least a hundred dollars each. Your three paints are worth to me, no more than forty dollars each. Prairie schooners are hard to come by but to be fair so is Pollyanna's little wagon. So I'll only charge you ten dollars for the swap. You can't use those cavalry saddles, they would be a dead giveaway if you get stopped by an Army patrol, so I'll give twenty dollars each for them. Taking everything into account I figure the difference to be, well, shall we say fifty dollars? Throw in your saddle horse, I guess you will want to keep its saddle, and let's say you owe me thirty dollars. I know you have the money; my message said you won it at poker in Clantonville. So do we have a deal, Major Hancock, or whatever your real name is?'

'Not quite. I need to keep my horse, besides he's not mine to sell. I only have the loan of him from the deputy sheriff of Clantonville and I'll need Pollyanna's saddle as well.'

The deputy sheriff of Clantonville was an old friend of Drury's, although he had not seen him for some time. Another idea began to form in his devious mind.

'Well, I can afford to be generous. Let's say another ten dollars and you can keep her saddle, even though it's not much use to her without a horse or pony to ride. Do we have a deal?'

'Yes, it seems I have little choice.'

Drury's eyes glinted at the possibility of another sale. Although they were perfectly sound, he had a couple of ponies he could not sell at any price.

'As for a steed for Pollyanna, I need all the horses I got. Business is good at the stable. However, I do have a couple of fine Indian ponies I'd be willing to let you have cheap.'

'Indian ponies?' queried Mike.

'Cayuse. Some say the breed was brought from Europe by the French Canadians but I ain't so sure. Pawnees have been breeding them for generations; I got a few as part of a deal some while back. Still got a couple left. One of them would make a perfect mount for your lady and the other a good packhorse.'

At that moment, an excited Polly brought the Shires and the big prairie schooner back into the main stable yard. It seemed Drury had not exaggerated for, even though they did not yet know her, both Shires had proved to be both remarkably friendly and very obedient.

Polly reluctantly handed the huge Shires and the prairie schooner back to a stable hand. Then Drury led Mike and Polly to a small corral at the rear of the stables.

In it were the cayuse. Polly joined them and gasped in amazement as she saw the two Indian ponies.

Seeing his chance to claim two more sales most probably lay with convincing Polly, Drury began to describe the cayuse in detail. He began with their size.

'The tallest cayuse, like these two, are about fourteen hands high at the shoulder, that's about the same size as the smallest mustang. Of course, the cayuse are ponies not horses. The Shires on the other hand are both just over eighteen hands high; the tallest breed of horses known to man,' he said proudly.

'Hands?' asked Polly, 'I haven't heard that term before.'

'One hand is about four inches in height,' chuckled Mike, pleased to show off his knowledge of horses.

'These cayuse are beautiful; are they all this colour, light reddish brown with manes and tails like pale gold?' asked Polly.

Drury laughed at Polly's romantic description of the two ponies. Realizing he now had her full attention, he continued with his sales pitch. So expert was he at this Polly didn't realize what he was doing.

'Horses are my passion as well as my livelihood,' he continued enthusiastically. 'I've read up on the different breeds and their normal colours whenever I could. Technically these are deemed to be chestnuts.'

'Their colour doesn't look anywhere near chestnut,' said Polly doubtfully.

'In horse terms, chestnut covers a variety of shades from pale or light brown, like these two I hope you are going to buy, to a dark, reddish-brown just like a real chestnut after it darkens after being exposed to prolonged sunlight,' said Drury in his most ingratiating manner.

'Mike, can we afford them as well?' asked Polly. In her excitement, she had used his real Christian name. A slip that later was to have dire consequences, but for now, Drury acted as if he hadn't noticed it.

'Fifty dollars the pair was the asking price but you can have them both for twenty dollars, providing your major keeps to the deal we've just concluded. Call it a going away present,' interrupted Drury before Mike could respond.

Taking into account his original deal for the cayuse ponies plus the cost of feeding, grooming and stabling them for the last three months, Drury stood to make a substantial loss on the sale. Unusually, he didn't care. The sale of the distinctive cayuse ponies was just part of an unscrupulous plan still developing in his devious mind.

To please Polly, Mike agreed to buy both Indian ponies. However, neither of them would be suitable to carry Jeff, who would also still need a horse to replace his paint. In buying the cayuses and completing the deal for the Shires and the prairie wagon, he used up a large part of their money. He tried to rationalize his decision by thinking that if along the Santa Fe trail they met hostile Indians, at least the women would have the means to escape. Unfortunately, ever the realist, he didn't really believe that, even mounted on the pair of cayuse ponies, the women would be able to outrun an Indian war party.

While he completed the paper work for the complex deal, Polly purchased more supplies with the last of *her* money. By the time they had been loaded into the prairie schooner, all the paperwork had been completed but it was too late to start back to her little spread. This suited

Drury so, making a show of what was entirely false generosity, he agreed to pay for their second night at the hotel and breakfast as well. Entirely false because, for reasons of his own, the longer he could delay Pollyanna and Major Hancock from leaving Smithville the better.

Because she had inadvertently used the major's real first name, Drury was sure the man in question was an impostor. Unfortunately, he needed help to turn that knowledge to his advantage; help that could only be provided by his friend, the deputy sheriff of Clantonville. But first he had to complete the sale of the paints to the Greys. There was nothing he could do that evening except inform his very able stable boy he would be away for a few days.

As lovers often do, Mike and Polly breakfasted late. By the time they had finished Drury was already at the Greys' stud ranch haggling over the price for the paints. In fact it was mid-morning before they left and in doing so they made an unusual sight. Mike, as usual, rode his borrowed bay horse while Polly drove the prairie schooner pulled with ease by two magnificent black Shires who towered over the cayuse ponies as they trotted alongside them.

Even so, they were long gone by the time Drury returned. He immediately banked the money from the sale of the paints, after which he had a late and leisurely lunch. Then, pausing only to pick up a fresh horse from his stable, he set off for Clantonville. However, as he couldn't swim he was not about to risk crossing the river even if its flood-swollen flow had abated. Instead, he rode south to the rail bridge. Then, having crossed the river, he turned north and headed to Clantonville.

This diversion added a few days to the trip. However, the delay didn't concern him for, after a brief conference with his old friend the deputy sheriff, it didn't take long to round up a posse and they left at dawn of the following day. However, neither he nor the deputy sheriff were in charge of the posse.

This role was taken by Major Allen. He had arrived in Clantonville a few days earlier. He informed Drury that, yes, they would be going after the impostor playing the role of Major Hancock but only because he was with Clara. He had information that although she had been thought to work for the Union, she had been actually a high-ranking Confederate spy. Major Allen also thought that there was more than a slight chance that a dangerous Reb prisoner, Jeff Kyle, an escapee from the train wreck, was with her.

None of which interested Drury in the slightest. Once the bogus major had been apprehended, or better still killed, he planned to let the deputy and the rest of the posse keep any reward for Hancock or the escaped Reb prisoner. He also expected that Major Allen would commandeer the prairie schooner. So be it. All Drury really wanted were the two Shires and Pollyanna. If he also got back the pretty little cayuse ponies so much the better, but they didn't really matter that much.

He planned to take Pollyanna back to her little spread and force her to succumb to his desires. She would have little choice in the matter. If she objected, once back in her isolated homestead, who then would hear her screams for help?

That pleasure was for the future. For now, after the drowning of Pollyanna's husband, none of the posse wanted to risk fording the river. Drury wholeheartedly agreed. But he insisted they took a spare set of horses so that they could change the ones they were riding as and when they tired. So, led by Major Allen, the posse headed south to the railway bridge, crossed it and then rode north towards Smithsville.

Drury was not at all concerned by the delay this second detour caused. If, as he supposed, the bogus major and Pollyanna intended to flee southwards towards the Confederate lines they would have to cross over the railway bridge since the ground on the other side soon became too rough for any sort of wagon to traverse. He half-expected to meet them either crossing the railway bridge or between it and Smithsville. But then Drury supposed that believing they were still safe from detection they might still be taking their ease in Smithville's one and only hotel, especially if the mysterious woman spy and the escaped Reb convict were with them.

Even the unlikely event of them having left Smithville and then heading north did not unduly worry Drury. The unusual combination of the large ebony-coloured Shires and the little light chestnut-coloured cayuse ponies with their golden manes and tails would be bound to attract attention in every settlement through which they passed. Moreover, although the Shires were extremely powerful they were built for strength not speed. With fresh horses to change to when the horses they were riding tired, Drury reckoned the posse would have little trouble in tracking down the prairie schooner.

CHAPTER TEN

THE MAYNARD CARBINES

Jeff Kyle had not been idle during Mike's absence. With Clara's help, he moved the bed, found the trapdoor and then opened it. A flight of steps descended into inky blackness. With the oil lamp illuminating his way, he clambered down the steps into a surprisingly large cellar. Its ceiling was well supported by solid wooden beams and the walls were lined with adobe. Even more surprisingly, there were several chairs, a table and a small cupboard that looked as if it may have once been used to store food and water. The trapdoor could be secured firmly from inside, suggesting that originally the cellar had been intended as a refuge against Indian attacks. That must have been a generation ago when the first settlers came to the area as most of the war-inclined, indigenous inhabitants had long since moved further west.

It was the combined pistol shelf and rifle rack in the corner of the cellar that caught Jeff's attention. In it were several old and dusty Confederate copies of the Springfield musket. The pistols in the rack were .44 calibre Colts, universally known as the Army type. Although they were Yankee pistols, Jeff had carried one that he had captured during his time with General Moseby. So he picked out the one that suited him the best and exchanged it for his Southern-made brass pistol.

The long guns in the crate were not rifles but the shorter-barrelled carbine. Brand new, they were still in their original factory wrappings. Unlike the single shot, muzzle-loading Springfield copies, these were breech loading. The trigger guard also doubled up as a lever; pulling it downwards and towards him caused the carbine's barrel to point downwards to enable reloading from the breech.

Jeff did not recognize the make; the engraved metal label on the left-hand side of the stock was little help; it only contained a series of patent numbers and a sign that read 'Manufactured by Mass. Arms Co. Chicopee Falls'.

That meant absolutely nothing to Jeff. Looking at the other side of the rifle's stock, it seemed that it too had once carried a plate but for some reason it had been removed. It was the same with the other carbines, six in all.

One by one, he carried the surprisingly light carbines up to the cabin's main living room and then carefully began to remove their protective coat of grease. However, it was self-evident they required a unique type of rim-edged cartridge and some sort of percussion cap to fire them. Without both of these the carbines were completely useless.

He was interrupted by the return of Clara. She had been collecting eggs to cook, a chore for which her life had left her ill prepared. During her childhood in Texas, she may have been something of a tomboy but she had never been allowed to cook and back east her aunt had considered any form of domestic labour to be beneath her niece.

'I've almost finished here. Would you like me to rustle up a meal?' asked Jeff putting aside the carbine he had just finished cleaning.

'It might be best, my kitchens skills are very limited,' admitted Clara.

'No problem, when I was a boy and, much to my father's amusement, I learnt to cook.'

'And yet you are an officer.'

'Was,' corrected Jeff. 'But yes, I graduated at West Point.'

'Sending you to West Point must have cost your parents plenty, so surely they could afford servants or did you have slaves?'

'No slaves, Father was an abolitionist but kept his views strictly to himself. He was a merchant, although only in a relatively small way. I guess we were neither rich nor poor, just comfortable enough off to afford a cook and a maid for my mother.'

In no time at all, Jeff whipped a few eggs, and found some stale cheese and the last rashers of bacon. To Clara's amazement, from these meagre ingredients he made a more than palatable omelette big enough for two.

Jeff then busied himself. Both his and Mike's pistols used 'roll your own' ammunition. Put simply, it was necessary to make the bullets before you could fire them. To the uninitiated this was a complicated business but Jeff had been making up his own bullets for many years. Clara was amazed at his dexterity and his patience as the pile of completed bullets grew and grew. So much so that by the time Avison and Polly returned he had filled several boxes. She too was amazed and asked why he had made so many bullets.

'Polly, I don't want to alarm you but it's a long, long way to Santa Fe and who knows what awaits us on the trail,' he explained.

Mike nodded in agreement, but Polly was not in the least deterred.

'You're not going to talk me out of coming with you, especially after . . .' Polly faltered and blushed deeply as she glanced across at Mike. The way he smiled back at her suggested to Clara that there had been a significant development in their relationship and she at once determined to find out whether her suspicions were well founded.

So when Polly suggested to Clara that they should take the prairie wagon for a short drive so she could learn to handle the magnificent Shires, she readily agreed. Jeff was too busy showing the mysterious breech-loading carbines to Avison to wonder at Clara's eagerness. Mike recognized the make if not the model.

'They're Maynard carbines, although I don't recognize the firing mechanism.'

'Explain,' said Jeff.

'At least a couple of Southern regiments used the

Maynard carbine. Way back I met a group of good old boys from Missouri who let me borrow one for a short time. I found it to be pretty accurate up to five hundred yards but it had one hell of a kick when fired. Strictly speaking, it's still a single shot like a musket but the Missouri men claimed that they could get off twelve shots per minute, although I never managed more than ten.'

'That's still three times more than the standard Springfield musket,' said Jeff.

'True, but there's a snag. It only fires a special cartridge patented by Maynard himself.'

'Pity. I searched the cellar but didn't find any,' said Jeff.

'That's because the powder and cartridges are in chests. They are buried under the outhouse. Do you think I was going to have them under my roof?' It was Polly, she had returned from driving the Shires and examining the Indian ponies. It had been only a brief trip because she did not yet want to discuss in detail her relationship with Mike.

It took an hour for Jeff and Mike to dig up the chests and Polly was right, they did contain all the necessary ingredients to make up a very considerable of quantity of bullets for the Maynard carbines. They also dug up a quite different long but narrow box. Jeff opened it to find it contained two very expensive-looking shot-guns. While he did so Mike examined the empty cartridge shells.

'Fifty calibre!' he exclaimed. 'These carbines must be a new version. The Maynard I borrowed fired .52 calibre. Perhaps the new carbines won't kick quite so badly as the old ones.'

'I've never seen cartridges like these. Do you reckon

they could be refilled and used more than once?' asked Jeff.

'Sure, the Missouri boys said they used them over and over again. Up to fifty times they claimed. Provided you managed to retrieve them once fired, of course!'

Although the discovery of the munitions was welcome, the cache caused some unforeseen problems. Not least being Polly's reluctance to have barrels of gunpowder sitting alongside the food supplies and the water barrels in the new wagon. So next day a council of war was held. After a long debate Clara came up with the solution.

'We need another wagon,' she said firmly.

'I don't think it wise for me go back to Smithsville. Drury is already suspicious of me,' said Mike.

'Even if we had the money, where else could we buy a wagon and horses to pull it?' asked Clara.

'I wasn't thinking of buying anything, just borrowing a rig from Clantonville. Wouldn't need to be anything fancy, just durable enough to last to Santa Fe,' said Clara.

'Mike, if you think this Drury fellow has become suspicious of you then I guess it's down to me,' said Jeff.

Mike nodded his head in agreement. Clara looked horrified but it was Polly who argued against the plan.

'Firstly, you've never been to Smithsville, so you won't know the best places to look for a suitable wagon. Then, even if you find one, which I doubt since the Union Army commandeered almost all of them, how are you going to *borrow* a team of horses and hitch them to the wagon on your own without being discovered?'

'There's another problem,' said Mike. 'Drury said the trail from here only leads back to Smithsville. So we can hardly *liberate* a wagon from there, return here to load it and then drive it back through there the next day.'

'We wouldn't have to. There's a bit of a trail northwards but it only goes as far as the Dawson spread. It's pretty overgrown because that spread has been abandoned since the early part of the war. Remember I said I grew up around here? When I was a little girl I used to be taken to play with the Dawson children,' said Polly.

'So what good would this trail do us?' asked Clara.

'Well, in normal times, even with a heavily loaded wagon it should be possible to cut across the Dawson spread and then head west, although with all the rainstorms we had recently it might not yet be possible,' said Polly.

'So how would that help us?' asked Jeff.

'It's a bit of a detour but we could join the main trail to Independence some miles north of Smithsville, so nobody there would be any the wiser.'

'Well, it would certainly give us a head start,' said Clara.

'Then first light tomorrow I'll scout the area,' said Mike.

'While you do, we could start loading the rest of the supplies into the prairie wagon,' said Clara.

'But we still need another wagon for the guns and ammunition,' said Polly determinedly.

CHAPTER ELEVEN

THE DESERTERS

Mike chose to wear his 'borrowed' officer's uniform. He wasn't sure if Drury had believed his story about being a scout and not needing to wear a military uniform, but he didn't want to take the risk with anyone else. It was a small decision but one destined to impact deeply on the future in ways that he could never have imagined.

The weather had almost returned to normal and it had not rained since they had first stumbled across Polly's spread. Nevertheless, the heat of the early morning sun still drew moisture out of the ground and that formed vast stretches of dense white mist. Many would have lost their way in such a mist but Mike was not one of them. Not for nothing had he been one of Jeb Stuart's top scouts. For him the dense white mist was an old and trusted friend who had often cloaked him from his enemies. And so it was this day.

Nevertheless, shrouded by the dense white mist, he

might have missed the trail to the Dawson ranch had it been actually abandoned. He didn't because it wasn't, abandoned that is. Recently formed horse cart tracks led him directly to the supposedly deserted ranch house.

A sudden gust of wind temporally parted the mist, revealing an outhouse in front of which was a wagon the like of which he had never seen before. There was no time to study it, however, for as the mist cleared further he could see the main building and standing outside its front door were two somewhat dishevelled-looking Union troopers. Had they looked in Mike's direction they must have seen him but, like the cavalry officers during his escape from the train wreck, they did not. Instead, they yawned and stretched suggesting to Mike that, although it was mid-morning, they had only just arisen.

But where were the sentries? Mike had almost blundered on a Yankee patrol without receiving a challenge from a sentry, even though he had made little attempt at stealth. He could not believe what he was seeing. These troopers, far from being alert, had struggled out of bed not at reveille but when they felt like it. So what sort of Yankee establishment was this? Mike had no idea but was determined to find out.

Two more soldiers wandered aimlessly out of the house and then from inside yet another called out to them. Were there any more? Mike couldn't tell because just at that movement the mist returned denser than ever, blanking out everything.

Mike used it to cover his retreat, but he did not go far. Just far enough to find a safe place to tether his horse. Then, under cover of the all-pervading mist, he returned to the Dawson establishment. Polly had said that the Dawsons were long gone, but what were the troopers doing here and where were their officers? Fortunately, the mist had thickened so much that Mike was able to get near enough to the house to hear most of what was being said. However, thick as the mist now was, the hot morning sun would almost certainly burn it away, so he could not risk a long stay.

From snippets of their conversation it soon became clear that the troopers were deserters and that was the reason no sentries had been posted. It seemed there were five of them in all and they were led by a corporal. But why had they deserted so near to the end of the Civil War and victory was assured for the Union?

There was, however, a more pressing problem to solve. Where were the deserters' horses? Using the cover of the still dense mist, Mike worked his way around the house, only to find its corral was empty.

From seemingly out of nowhere came a breeze. It began to swirl the mist around and through a gap Mike saw a barn about fifty paces away. In it he could hear horses, so he silently approached the barn and entered. Taking care not to disturb the horses, which were already restless, Mike searched the rest of the barn. Apart from some hay the only other item of interest he found was a saddle. That could only mean that one of the horses was used to being ridden while the other four must have been trained to pull the strange-looking cart. But which one? It didn't take Mike, who had been around horses all his life, long to find out.

This morning luck was on Mike's side for it couldn't have

worked out better; another saddle horse meant there would be one each for himself and Jeff; the cart that Polly wanted and horses trained to pull it. If needed, the girls could ride the Indian ponies. There was just the little matter to resolve; getting the horses and wagon away from the Dawson ranch. The five desperate Union deserters were not about to part with them without one hell of a fight.

Mike had identified at least five deserters and there were almost certainly more inside the ranch house; far too many for Mike to handle alone. But how long did they intend to stay at the Dawson ranch? He had to find out. Outside the barn the heat of the sun was beginning to thin the white mist, so he had to leave soon. Then, raised voices from inside the house suggested the deserters were arguing about the very thing Mike most wanted to know about them.

The smell of cooking bacon suggested they were about to eat breakfast. It seemed reasonable to suppose the deserters were not about to leave the house until they had eaten. So Mike crept under the half-open window and eavesdropped on all fours.

'I say we should use the mist and make a run for it,' said one of the deserters.

'I'm for that,' said another. 'This damned fog has been here as long as we have. Perhaps it never goes away.'

'No wonder the place is deserted. Who'd want to live in a place like this? Finish your breakfast boys while I go and hitch up the horses,' said another voice.

Alarmed at the prospect of certain discovery, Mike began to move away but then from inside the house came a dissenting voice.

110

'Sit down, Briggs. Last time I looked I was the one wearing the stripes.'

'We've left the Army, corporal, or are we on some sort of special patrol?' retorted the man called Briggs. His retort caused much merriment among the other troopers, but the corporal swiftly reasserted his authority.

'Patrol? I'll give you patrols!' he shouted. 'Think about it, if you can. Our ex comrades will have dozens of patrols looking for those two bloody Reb spies who escaped from the train wreck. If we run into them, how are you going to fight them off with just four Springfield muskets and two Army Colts? Or do you propose to outrun them in the wagon?'

'You're right, Corps,' said one of the other deserters, 'I guess we had better listen to you.'

'Too right you had, my boys. Remember, we killed that officer to get away, so it's the firing squad for all of us if we get caught.'

'So, *corporal*, what do you suggest we do?' The voice was heavily laced with sarcasm, as was the emphasis placed on the rank of their leader. However, the man in question hit back hard.

'I don't suggest nothing. I tells you we stay here. We got food and water and beds to sleep in ain't we? And if you're bored then, after breakfast you can go and rub down the horses like proper soldiers do.'

Mike had heard enough and crept away. He reached his horse as just the sun began to break through the mist. Within minutes the dense mist had gone but by then Mike was well on his way. He had much to tell the others, including how he intended to raid the Dawson ranch. However, over dinner, that part of his plan went down like a lead balloon. Polly in particular objected to his plan; so did Jeff and he had a strong case.

'Mike, I don't doubt your ability as a scout or that you can more than look after yourself, you've proven that many times since we met. But apart from the Shires, which are far too big to ride, we've only one horse between us. In any case, raiding the Dawson ranch should be my job.'

'How come?' asked Clara sharply.

'I rode with Moseby's Irregulars and raided dozens of Yankee strongholds. So much so, it's almost second nature to me now.'

'But single you can't take on five soldiers on your own,' said Clara.

'If we're to get out of here, one of us will have to,' said Mike grimly.

'Perhaps not,' said Polly. . . .

While Polly outlined her plan, many miles away Drury rode into Clantonville.

CHAPTER TWELVE

MASSACRE AT DAWSON'S RANCH

It was almost dawn but the morning mist that always seemed to engulf the Dawson ranch was not quite as thick as usual. On an impulse that was later to serve him well, Mike was again wearing the uniform of Major Hancock. It had been freshly washed and ironed by Polly. Jeff was still in his Reb's uniform, which was beginning to look decidedly the worse for wear. Together, they silently approached the ranch house.

In spite of all their objections, they had not been allowed to travel on their own. Armed with a six-gun and roughly a mile to the east of the ranch were Polly and Clara. It had been Polly's idea to drive their newly acquired prairie schooner to within a reasonable walking distance of the supposedly abandoned Dawson spread. However, in spite of Polly and Jeff's objections, at her

113

shoulder and still dressed in men's clothes sat Clara. With her hair tucked under a Stetson that had once belonged to Polly's late husband and a six-gun tucked into the top of her britches, from a distance she made a passable impression of a young ranch hand. The loaded shot-gun she held, one of the pair found by Jeff in Polly's cellar, helped to complete the illusion.

In spite of their weaponry, both girls were very nervous. Perhaps that was why Polly spoke so openly about her relationship with Mike. If Clara was more reticent about showing her feelings towards Jeff, she didn't fool Polly for a moment.

'You care for him, don't you?' she asked.

Clara blushed and hesitated before answering.

'Yes, I believe I do. Not that he's shown any interest towards me in that way,' she added hastily.

'Of course not. Jeff's an officer and too much of a gentleman to do so without a certain amount of encouragement. Mike may not have been an officer but he too was a perfect gentleman until in Smithsville I tricked him into sharing a bedroom with me. Even then without a lot of inducement from me, he would not have taken advantage of the situation. Can you believe he actually intended to sleep in a chair beside my bed?'

'But you've only just met. How can you be so sure of him?' asked Clara.

'I'm not. He may yet leave me when we get to Independence or after we reach Santa Fe. After all he's a scout, so living under the stars and moving from town to town is in his nature. It's down to me to make him want to settle down. . . .'

114

Dawn failed to disperse the dense mist, allowing Mike to make his way to the barn unobserved. The horses were still in there but the strange-looking wagon was on the other side of the house, making it impossible to harness the horses to it without disturbing the deserters. So he returned to the place where Jeff was waiting for him.

'Can't get the horses hitched to the wagon without disturbing the deserters so we have to attack them. There can be no quarter given, they must not get past us, *our* girls are only a mile away,' said Mike.

'Agreed, after all the deserters are Yankee soldiers and we are still at war. Fortunately for us they've been damned careless, the side widow shutter hasn't been closed properly. So I'll go in that way. You cover the front door,' said Jeff.

'Yes lieutenant,' said Mike, acknowledging this was Jeff's show. 'Just don't get yourself killed. Your Clara would never forgive me.'

However the chance to put Jeff's plan into action was denied them, for out of the mist on the other side of the house came a hail.

'You deserters in the house, give yourself up.'

Out of the mist, and led by a very young-looking officer brandishing his sabre, emerged a small group of Union soldiers. Although they were clearly cavalry men, they were all on foot. The newness of their uniforms suggested to both Mike and Jeff that these troops were new to actual combat. This joint opinion was confirmed when the troops drew their sabres and, led by the youthful lieutenant, charged towards the house in what appeared to be a well-rehearsed drill. However, this was not a drill.

'Damned fools, they will be cut to pieces,' growled Mike.

And so it proved. Whatever they had now become, the deserters proved to be battle-seasoned soldiers. So they held their fire until the lieutenant and his men had almost reached the ranch house front door. Although the deserters' volley was ragged, they could hardly miss the troopers at such close range; all four musket shots found their target. But the rest of the troopers reached the front door. Led by their lieutenant, they charged through it, only to be met by pistol fire from the two deserters carrying side-arms.

The mist swirled down, obscuring Mike and Jeff's view, but they could hear several shots, blood-curling shouts and screams as the fight continued. Then, there was nothing except silence.

A few moments later the mist parted, revealing a grizzly and macabre scene. Although two of the deserters lay dead, the inexperienced troopers had been massacred. Slumped over two prone bodies was the young lieutenant. He had lost his sabre and his pistol lay on the ground beside him. Wounded and distraught by the loss of his men, he was clearly in no condition to defend himself.

It seemed to Jeff that the deserters had decided to finish him off. Indeed, they were in such a hurry they made the fatal mistake of not stopping to reload their muskets. Instead, bayonets fixed, they rushed towards the stricken man.

Mike had seen enough and opened fire. His Maynard carbine spat death as one of the deserters fell to the ground. Jeff also fired but, unused to the Maynard, his bullet went wide of the mark. It didn't matter. Mike opened the breech of his carbine, reloaded and fired before any of the other deserters could take cover. As before, he didn't miss.

Taking only a few seconds longer than Mike to reload, Jeff fired again. A fast learner, his next shot struck home. He then reloaded his Maynard carbine almost as quickly as Mike. They fired almost simultaneously; in a matter of seconds, all the deserters who had charged out of the Dawson ranch house were dead.

Cautiously, Jeff and Mike approached the carnage. Barely ten minutes had elapsed since the troopers had recklessly charged the house. Now, they were all dead, only their lieutenant had survived and even he seemed to be wounded. However, there were still some deserters in the house. Jeff drew his six-gun, motioned to Mike to remain where he was and then disappeared into the swirling mist.

Mike cursed silently as the mist again thickened. There was nothing he could do but wait. He did not have to wait for long. Three shots rang out almost simultaneously and then silence. But had Jeff or the deserters survived? A reassuring hail from the house told Mike that Jeff had been the sole victor of the gunfight.

The strengthening breeze began to blow the mist away. As it did so Mike could see dead bodies sprawled out in front of him. However, both he and Jeff were seasoned campaigners and both had seen worse scenes of carnage, not least at the train wreck. So relatively unconcerned, Jeff from the ranch house and Mike from his place of hiding, walked through the dead bodies until they converged on the young union lieutenant.

He was not dead. A bullet had grazed his temple, temporarily stunning him, while another had nicked his ear lobe, causing it to bleed profusely even though it was only a minor wound. He was the enemy but even after four years of bitter war neither Mike nor Jeff could bring themselves to shoot a defenceless man. However, they could not take him prisoner and Jeff's Confederate uniform posed a problem.

'Jeff, leave this to me. Before this Yankee lieutenant comes round get yourself into the barn and keep out of sight until I get him into the ranch house. Then, while I keep him occupied, hitch up the wagon and drive it back to *our* girls. Don't wait for me, head straight back to Polly's spread. I should catch up with you long before you reach it but in case I don't, start packing straight away,' ordered Mike.

'You think there are more Yankee troops about?' asked Jeff.

'Yes, and they will be certain to see your wagon tracks. I want us all to be well away from Polly's spread before they or anyone else reaches it.'

'So you think the Clantonville posse is still after us?' asked Jeff.

'Yes Jeff, I do.'

'But that doesn't make sense. Polly's husband escaped from Clantonville and then was drowned trying to cross the river. Surely he wouldn't have tried to do so unless the posse's jurisdiction ended on the other side of the river?' said Jeff.

'Maybe. But I don't think it's us the deputy sheriff is

really after. I think it's to do with the key Clara took off me at gunpoint when we first met. Take care Jeff, there's more to that lady than meets the eye. She's a beauty to be sure but remember, Shakespeare once wrote "all that glisters is not gold." '

'I didn't realize you studied Shakespeare,' said Jeff, suitably impressed.

'There's a lot you don't know about me but as I said to you once before, this ain't the time for my life story.'

'So what are you going to do with him?' asked Jeff as the lieutenant began to stir.

'Nothing unless he leaves me no other choice. I'll just bluff it out and pull the same trick I used after the train crash. After all, I got a lot more practice at being a Union major since then when I pretended you were my prisoner. So unless you want me to knock you out again, skedaddle into the barn, pronto.'

Jeff did as he was bid, but he was not a second too soon. He had only just disappeared into the barn when the lieutenant recovered consciousness.

Seeing what he immediately assumed to be a superior officer, the lieutenant tried to stand up to deliver his report but staggered as he spoke.

'Sir, I'm Lieutenant Brown. . . .'

'Easy now, lieutenant. You've had a narrow shave. Let's go into the kitchen and then while you're recovering, I'll brew us some coffee,' said Mike, again assuming the role of Major Hancock.

While Mike did so, Jeff as quietly as it is possible to be with a group of horses, took the four unsaddled ones from the barn and then hitched them to the strange-looking

wagon. Even so, had the Yankee lieutenant not been con-
cussed or too shocked by the loss of all his men he must
have noticed the wagon as Jeff drove it past the ranch
house and into the mist, which had returned with a
vengeance.

The lieutenant's report was brief but to the point. He
had been leading his men on a patrol searching for the
deserters but had lost his way in the mist. It had been
purely by chance they had stumbled across the Dawson
ranch, which he had been told was deserted. Finding that
it wasn't, he correctly guessed it had been occupied by the
deserters. As a result he had then issued the standard challenge but had received no reply.

Straight out of the academy, this had been his first
command, he had done everything by the training manual
and ordered his troopers to dismount. Then, sabre drawn,
he had led his men towards the ranch house. As a result
they had been slaughtered by the deserters, who had been
war-seasoned soldiers. Fortunately for him, but much to
his shame, while all the men under his command had
been slain, the lieutenant's wounds, although causing him
to temporarily lose consciousness, were relatively minor.

'Sir, I never thought the deserters would open fire on
their fellow troopers,' he confessed bitterly.

'You're not the first officer to have his command wiped
out and I guess you won't be the last,' said Mike.

'Perhaps not, sir, but I'll be court-martialled for sure. I
cannot deny that it's my fault my men are dead, so the best
I can hope for is a dishonourable discharge.'

'It was the deserters who shot your men. Had they not
deserted this massacre could not have happened, so they

alone are responsible for your men's deaths. Now, if I can find some writing material, I'll write a report to that effect and you can take it back with you,' said Mike still playing the role of Major Hancock for all his worth.

'Thank you, sir, but will you not be riding back to Independence with me?'

'No, lieutenant, my orders demand otherwise.'

After a surprisingly short search, Mike found both pen and paper. Just as he had done at the train wreck, he wrote out a series of orders for a young Yankee lieutenant to carry out. Only this time he added a description of the massacre at the Dawson ranch, exonerating Lieutenant Brown from any blame for the death of his men. Mike reasoned that as the war was almost over, even though he was the enemy, there was no need for the young lieutenant to carry a condemnation on his record that would blight the rest of his life. It was an act of charity that was to have far-reaching repercussions.

A few minutes later the lieutenant rode into the mist, grateful to be alive and even more grateful to have the written approbation of his actions tucked into his tunic. Mike waited until he was sure the lieutenant was not coming back and picked out the best of the Army horses, two fine black stallions.

Two because it was time to get rid of the horse he had 'borrowed' from Clantonville. Although it had been loaned to him by its deputy he had nothing in writing to that effect. Even if he denied that he had stolen the beast, no one would believe him and horse stealing was a hangable offence. The second stallion was, of course, for Jeff so that he could share in the scouting duties during

121

the trek to Independence.

Confident that the other Army horses would not roam too far, he set about unsaddling and untethering them. He also did the same for the horses belonging to the deserters. The Yankees were bound to return to the Dawson ranch to bury their dead, so chasing after their horses in the mist and fog might keep them occupied for an extra day or so; time Mike meant to put to good use.

As the mist finally lifted, Mike, leading the other black Army stallion, rode away from the scene of the massacre. He neither looked back nor gave another thought about the dead men; four years of bloody warfare hardens even the best of men.

CHAPTER THIRTEEN

MOMENTOUS TIDINGS

Even from a mile away Clara and Polly heard most of the gunshots. That there had been so many convinced them that Mike and Jeff had ridden into a trap. In her mind Clara pictured Jeff's body lying on the ground riddled with bullets. So when he appeared driving the odd-looking wagon her relief so overwhelmed her that she burst into tears. But there was no sign of Mike. Polly bit her lip and kept silent. She was pleased to see Jeff but she was not about to spoil the reunion by revealing how worried she was about Mike. However, she didn't fool anyone.

'Mike's fine,' said Jeff and then briefly explained what had happened.

Polly could not disguise the look of relief that spread over her face. Even so, it was a sombre party that slowly headed back to Polly's spread. During the trip Jeff began to plan the long trek ahead while Polly pondered over the best way to pack the odd-looking wagon Jeff was now driving.

Clara had been on her own for so long she had become quite reconciled to the feeling of loneliness. It was part of the price she had willingly paid for her espionage work. She had been a far more important spy than any of her companions realized, as had been the man also playing the role of Major Hancock; for in spite of his blue uniform and his poor poker playing, he too had been a Confederate sympathizer. He too had been an impostor. The real Major Hancock was actually languishing in a Confederate prison camp and had been there for over a year.

Together, the first impostor and Clara had planned an escape route back to the Confederacy in the event of their detection or, as now seemed more than likely, the defeat of the South. So when Mike Avison arrived also posing as the major she had latched on to him, intending to use him as her means of escape from Union agents, who she knew would eventually track her down.

At gunpoint, when Mike had been posing as Hancock, she had taken a key from him. That key opened a strong-box stored in a vault in Independence, so she couldn't believe her luck when Polly had suggested they should go there. In the strongbox was a list of Confederate sympathizers who had been operating high in the Union government ranks. Her last mission was to destroy that list before it got into Union hands.

She also knew that the strongbox contained sufficient Yankee money to re-establish herself in society and so net a fine husband. But since she had met Jeff that latter ambition was no longer her goal.

Her ever-growing feelings for Jeff and the dread she felt when she heard the gunshots from the Dawson ranch had left her mind in turmoil. Yet she could not let her feelings towards him jeopardize her carefully laid out plan. Or could she? Her mind told her one thing, her heart quite the opposite.

Yet Jeff's attention while driving the other wagon seemed not to be directed towards her. He had never tried to kiss her, nor had he given her any reason to believe he returned the special feelings she now felt for him. Yet she could not abandon him or her two new friends when they reached Independence; she wanted to feel Jeff's embrace more and more.

Much to Polly's relief, Mike, leading the other black Army stallion, soon rejoined them. Fortunately, the rest of the return journey was uneventful. Tired, in spite of the need to quit Polly's spread as soon as possible, they decided to leave packing until the morning. While the men fed and groomed the horses Polly, perhaps more hindered than helped by Clara, prepared a sumptuous dinner for each of them. As Mike had said, during their journey to Independence it might not always be possible to enjoy a cooked meal.

Much of the supplies had been removed from the prairie wagon in preparation for its use in the raid on the deserters. So after breakfast next morning, they began to repack it.

However, only the prairie wagon had a permanent cover, so it was decided that beds for the girls would be laid in it. The wagon taken from the deserters was an entirely different affair. Clearly, it had been used as an Army supply wagon and several modifications had been made to it. The most useful as far as Mike was concerned was the addition of two forty-five gallon beer barrels strapped securely to each side of the wagon. However, both barrels were empty. Loading them with fresh water using one small pail and various kitchen utensils was a very slow process. . .

While the four were busy filling the two water barrels, a posse finally rode out of Clantonville led by Major Allen. The deputy sheriff rode with it, as did Drury, who was now acting as deputy sheriff of Smithsville.

Some said Allen had been working behind Confederate lines in some sort of secret role; he neither denied nor confirmed the rumour. All he would say was that his main interest lay in apprehending the woman they were now certain was a key double agent passing important information to the Rebs.

Major Allen had a formidable presence, with piercing eyes, a long black beard and moustache. When he was angry or vexed, which was quite often, he lapsed into a guttural accent that some said was Glaswegian. Allen himself would not be drawn as to his place of birth.

'We're not here to discuss my private life but to catch a dangerous Confederate spy,' he growled.

However, that was not strictly accurate. Allen had explicit written instructions since it was not actually Clara he wanted. It was the key to the strong box she was carrying that was the real purpose of the chase.

Clara knew of Allen's involvement in her affairs and of his formidable reputation. She was only too well aware that he would pursue her relentlessly and that if he caught her he would have her shot as a spy. Unsurprisingly, she was frustrated that packing the two wagons had taken so long that Mike had decided not to start out until the following day.

'We will all be better for another hot meal and a good night's sleep. Might be some time before you girls sleep in a real bed again,' he said.

There was no gainsaying that. Yet for one reason or another none of them slept well, although in spite of her fears of capture it was thoughts of Jeff that kept Clara awake. Before they reached Independence she determined to find out what if any feelings he had for her. Whatever it took.

While she had no regrets at leaving her home, Polly was nevertheless worried about her future. Fears of what might or might not happen constantly interrupted her sleep.

While the girls slumbered fitfully, Jeff and Mike tried to plan against any unforeseen problems. But there were too many variables, so after an hour or so they gave up.

'Best take it one day at a time,' said Mike. 'I think it best I do most of the scouting while you stay near the wagons.'

'Agreed, I'll sort out some suitable weapons for our two ladies,' replied Jeff.

'Fine, but look out for Clara's derringer. In fact, Jeff, as I said before, watch out for that lady. My scouting instincts have kept me safe most of the time and although I like her, something about her doesn't ring quite true.'

'In what way?' asked Jeff.

'I wish I could say for sure. When we first met I was, of course, posing as Major Hancock. Although she knew I wasn't him, she didn't give me away and only seemed interested in the key I had taken off his body. Yet she's never mentioned it once since then, although she keeps it attached to the necklace she always wears.'

'Not much to go on,' said Jeff,

'No, except she seems a trifle too eager to get to Independence. Hell, I may be wrong. Just use your head and not your heart where she's concerned.'

'I've hardly looked at her,' protested Jeff.

'Yeah, like I believe that. In any case, I've noticed the way she looks at you,' said Mike laughingly as he went to check the wagons. There was, however, a gentle warning behind his mirth.

Very early next morning, before Clara had risen, Polly began to cook a massive breakfast using all the supplies not packed in the wagons. They all ate their fill and then just after dawn they set out.

Gentle as the giant Shires had proven to be, they were not about to follow another wagon. Unbidden by Polly, and with the loosely tethered cayuse ponies following behind, the giant Shires trotted on until they had established the lead over the wagon driven by Jeff. Not that he minded. Driving four horses meant controlling four separate reins, one for each horse. Unfortunately, that was about the only thing about horses he had not been taught during his time serving under the Grey Fox in the 43rd Irregulars. Driving a four-in-hand was much harder than he thought and it took his entire concentration.

Fortunately, the black Army stallions selected for him by Mike had been so well trained they needed no tether and obediently trotted with the two cayuse ponies beside the ex-Army wagon.

Clara then opted to ride with Polly so that from time to time she could help out with the driving. Meanwhile, Mike scouted the trail ahead. They made steady progress until they hit the dense white mist that had enveloped the Dawson ranch since the great storm.

For the men, the mist was once again a blessing. It meant that they could drive though the Dawson ranch without the girls seeing the dead bodies now grotesquely distorted by rigor mortis, but Mike had another reason.

One of the deserters was approximately the same size as Jeff and he removed the deserter's tunic and replaced it with his own, neither an easy or pleasant job. Although rigor mortis had set in and almost made the movement of the dead man's limbs impossible, it had done nothing to alleviate the stench of death. Yet he got the job done and they left as quickly as the all-pervading mist would permit.

Whilst the mist had prevented the girls from seeing the dead bodies, it had kept the ground moist, and moist ground leaves tracks, especially when wagons are heavily laden. Unfortunately, there was little Mike could do about it as there were so many tracks it would take hours to cover them up. It was time Mike judged would be better spent heading towards Independence.

He was only partly right. Although Major Allen and his posse had already crossed the river, they had used the railway bridge to do so. Of course, this crossing was much further south than the one made by Mike, Jeff and Clara. Consequently, their route to Smithsville passed well south of Polly's old homestead.

Drury was surprised to find that Clara and the man he knew as Major Hancock had not yet accepted his invitation to stay in the settlement's only hotel. He wrongly assumed that they were taking their time in loading the wagon. Major Allen made no such assumption, nor did he buy into the idea that the wagon would be travelling south.

'I've come across this Clara woman before. She's a top Confederate agent so she wouldn't be so stupid as to give away the direction in which they intend to head.'

But Drury wouldn't listen.

'Listen to me, Major Allen. You're completely wrong. The woman with this Hancock imposter is Pollyanna Cooper, a young widow, her husband was drowned trying to cross that damned river. I've known her for years, she can't be this Clara you keep going on about.'

'Yet when Clara left Clantonville she left on Hancock's paint, and your stable lad said Pollyanna rode a paint.'

'Yes I know; I bought it plus two others from Hancock. He had the bill of sale for them.'

Armed with that information, Major Allen set out for Pollyanna's spread next morning. Much to his disgust, Drury was forced to go with them. He had wanted to ride south but the major had said no. So instead, Drury found himself leading the major and his posse to Polly's spread. Of course, they found it deserted. Worse still, the ground was covered by so many tracks criss-crossing each other that it was impossible to tell whether they had been made by wagons approaching the homestead or leaving it.

Before they finally left Polly's home, Mike, using all of his experience as a former scout, had spent time making sure of that.

Yet Mike's handy work made no difference. Drury knew the area almost as well as Pollyanna and instinctively knew where she and the man masquerading as Major Hancock were heading.

'They will be heading north. My guess is that they intend to hide out in the Dawson ranch; it's been deserted since old man Dawson died of the fever. Nobody ever goes there now,' said Drury, thinking out aloud.

'Well, you could be right,' said one of the posse doubtfully.

'If they had headed west towards Smithsville we would have run into them,' said Drury.

'East takes them back to the river,' said another posse member, 'which they couldn't cross in a wagon, and they won't have gone south for fear of running into the cavalry patrols that are still searching for the Reb outfit that attacked the train carrying the prisoners.'

'You're all right,' agreed Allen. 'So everyone mount up and then Mr Drury can lead us to this abandoned ranch.'

Riding as hard as the horses could manage, Drury led the posse until the cloying mist and the sickening stench of death greeted them. Even so, as they rode out of the mist they were completely taken aback by the horror that lay in front of the Dawson ranch. There were more than a dozen bodies, all but one of them clad in blue Union tunics. The other, a Reb officer, wore grey.

The prostrate bodies, rigid as grotesque stone statues due to the onset of rigor mortis, were beset by flies. If that was not bad enough, many of them, including the lone Reb, had been severely mutilated by coyotes. The stench was so horrific that most of the posse began to retch violently.

'Dismount and pull yourselves together. Go find spades, shovels or anything thing else to dig with. You've bodies to move out of sight of the ranch house. Then, when you've found a suitable site, bury them,' ordered Major Allen.

Although they searched thoroughly, the posse could only find two spades and a couple of shovels. Nevertheless, they set to work with a will, no doubt thinking the sooner the bodies were moved and buried the sooner they would be able to able to get away from the ranch and the foul smell that engulfed it.

One of the posse whose grisly job had been to search the corpses approached Allen.

'These papers were on the Reb's body,' he said.

Major Allen took them. The papers appeared to identify the dead Confederate officer as Lieutenant Jeff Kyle.

Jeff had, of course, exchanged his grey Reb uniform with the corpse, a Union trooper. Even for a hard-bitten veteran of the war, changing uniforms with the mutilated body had been a grizzly and thoroughly unpleasant task. Nevertheless, it had to be done if he was to have any chance of avoiding the hangman's noose. He had then left the papers in the dead man's pocket in the hope that whoever found them would assume that the corpse was Jeff.

Fortunately for Jeff, he had never been on Allen's capture list. Nevertheless, had the corpse not been so badly mutilated by coyotes a more thorough examination might then have taken place, which would have almost certainly led to the discovery of the charade.

'Well, that's one job less for the hangman,' said Allen.

Moving the bodies was a grim and grizzly task. Then, despite the softness of the moist earth, the posse, hampered by the lack of enough proper tools, the mass burial took almost three hours.

Had the posse but known it, when they arrived at the Dawson ranch they had only missed Jeff and Mike's little wagon train by an hour. Indeed, had the posse headed southwards immediately after their grisly task had been completed they could not have missed their tracks cut deep into the soft ground. But as the mist gave way to torrential rain they did not. Instead, seeing that his men were soaked to the skin, exhausted and sickened by the burial of so many mutilated bodies, Allen decided to return to Smithville.

His intention was, after a good night's rest for both his men and their horses to resume the pursuit of Clara. However, early next morning a Union trooper, his horse steaming with sweat after a hard night's ride, rode into Smithville. He was looking for Major Allen and found him having breakfast at the hotel.

'Urgent dispatch for you, sir,' he said, handing Allen sealed orders.

Allen broke the seal and opened it. In fact, there were two separate documents. The first read:

By command of General Ulysses Grant, Commander of the Army of the Potomac.

By way of explanation the second document simply read:

On April 9th General Lee, Confederate Commander-in-Chief of the Northern Virginia Army, signed a Surrender Treaty at Appomattox Courthouse, Virginia. On the following day, details of the actual surrender were finalised at the Commissioners Meeting.

Major Allen made public the news and word of Lee's surrender spread like wildfire. The citizens of Smithville quickly arranged a celebratory party and dance for that evening. However, there were a few dissenting voices. One of them was Drury.

'But there are still other Reb armies out there?' he said.

'Several,' agreed Allen, 'but Lee was the natural leader, the heart and soul of the South's main army, so it's reasonable to assume the other Reb factions such as their independent Partisan armies will soon follow his lead.'

The celebrations lasted into the early hours of next morning. Yet as dawn broke, half a dozen riders led by Drury and what was now with the coming of peace the former deputy of Clantonville galloped out of Smithville and headed north along the main trail to Independence.

CHAPTER FOURTEEN

HOT PURSUIT

Clara, unaware of the momentous events at Appomattox Courthouse in Virginia, fretted at the delay in starting out. Subconsciously, she fingered the key hanging on the necklace around her neck. It was the only one left that could open a trunk stored in a vault deep under the ground of the smallest bank in Independence.

That was all she knew about the trunk's whereabouts. Nevertheless, she was confident she could find it. She was anxious to discover what mysteries it held apart from the list of secret Confederate sympathizers who held influential posts in the Union government. It was her duty to destroy that list but the rest of the trunk's contents were hers to keep or share with her companions, and that decision bothered her.

Or to be more precise, Jeff bothered her. Did he have

any special feelings towards her at all? If he did, he was covering them up very well. Even if he had feelings for her would they be strong enough to make him want to go east to enable her to return to her old life? And if he did, what work could he then do? She feared that he would be like a fish out of water in the society in which she had intended to live.

On the other hand, if he really cared for her could she settle down in the west with him? Why not? After all, she was a Texas-born girl and proud of it. But there was a whole heap of difference in being brought up on a vast ranch where she had wanted for nothing to eking out a living on some isolated homestead. Could she do that? Yes, but only if Jeff asked her. Unfortunately, as yet, he had given no indication that he was going to do so. In fact, from the start of the trek to Innocence he seemed to have gone out to his way to avoid her.

For instance, it was decided that the girls would drive the wagons to allow Jeff and Mike to scout the trail in front and behind of them. Polly had no trouble in handling the two great shires. However, although she had been born on a great Texas ranch, Clara had never driven a prairie schooner. Yet it was Mike not Jeff who sat with her as she gradually learned to control the individual reins of each horse. As there were now six of them, it was no mean task.

So it was no surprise that at first their progress was slow. They headed north towards the Dawson ranch, then turned westward and two days later picked up the main trail to Independence.

For several days they continued west through the flat featureless landscape without meeting anyone, so they knew nothing of Lee's surrender and the effective end of the Civil War. They plodded on without incident until the first range of albeit small hills they had seen since leaving Polly's spread came in sight. Then, Mike, who had been scouting the trail behind them, came galloping up to the wagons with the news that Clara had long dreaded.

'At least six riders are heading this way. I was too far away to be sure but at least two or three of them looked like men from the Clantonville posse.'

'Did they see you and how long before they catch up with us?' asked Jeff.

'Of course they didn't see me; I used to be a scout. Besides, they were too busy dismounting and hobbling their horses to notice anybody. I guess they were intending to eat while their horses rested and grazed. But they didn't unsaddle them or light a fire, so I don't expect them to remain camped for long. Say two hours at most.'

'How far behind us are they?' asked Clara anxiously.

'Once they get started, no more than an hour's hard ride,' said Mike grimly.

'I don't understand. Why they are they still chasing us? Surely we have long passed out of their jurisdiction?' asked Jeff.

'It's me they are after, not you,' admitted Clara.

'It wouldn't be anything to do with the key you took from me at gunpoint on the night we first met in Clantonville?' asked Mike astutely.

'Yes, Mike, it is. I've put you all into danger,' Clara admitted contritely.

'So what's so important about this key?' asked Polly.

'With the war almost lost, I was ordered to go to

Independence and destroy the contents of a chest containing documents listing people in influential positions in the Yankee government who were actually Confederate sympathizers.'

'Is that the only reason you've been riding with us?' asked Polly.

'No, although it was the reason I didn't give Mike away to the Yankees when he was posing as Major Hancock, there's another reason I've stayed with you,' Clara said, blushing profusely.

Of course, Polly knew and Mike guessed what that reason was but as yet Jeff hadn't the faintest idea. Instead, he asked an obvious question.

'If we had decided to head south through the Indian Badlands and on to Texas, would you have come with us?'

'No, Jeff. In that case my duty to the Confederate cause would have taken precedent over my personal wishes and I would have travelled on my own to Independence if there had been no other alternative. I'm sorry I deceived you all. If I had the chance to redo the past I would have told you about my mission from the beginning.'

There were tears in her eyes as she spoke that even Jeff noticed.

'No problem, you didn't know us then or that we're all on the same side,' he said huskily.

'But I guess the riders behind us are not, so let's get the wagons rolling,' said Mike.

'Can we outrun them?' asked Polly.

'Not a chance. Our only hope is to head for those hills. Jeff, as my horse is spent, I'll take yours and ride on ahead and see if I can find somewhere we can make a stand,' replied Mike.

Without another word, he rode away but although time was at a premium he rode at a canter not at a gallop. He had already ridden his own steed to the point of exhaustion and did not want to repeat the process with Jeff's.

For the first time on this journey, Jeff sat beside Clara and drove the wagon. As he urged the horses into a canter there was an uncomfortable silence between them. For his part, it was due to him concentrating on the driving.

As soon the horses began to blow, Jeff reduced the pace to little more than walking speed. However, the Shires pulling the wagon driven by Polly refused to drop their pace and trotted with contemptuous ease past Jeff driving the prairie schooner. Normally, the giant Shires were obedient, but as natural leaders in the world of horses, they hated following others of their kind. Indeed, in spite of Polly's repeated instructions, they refused to slow down until they were sure that the horses pulling the prairie schooner were not going to overtake them.

As they drove slowly towards the still distant hills Clara began to pluck up the courage to unburden her heart to Jeff. However, before she could do so he pre-empted her.

'Do you think you could unpack and then load the Maynard carbines and get me the Springfield musket? They're in the back of the other wagon,' he said.

'Of course, Jeff, if that's what you want.'

'What I want? Not really. It's just that we have to be prepared to fight. If my own circumstances were what they used to be, then, it might be different. But they're not. Unfortunately, they are what they are,' he said mysteriously.

Clara longed to question Jeff further but there was no time. The posse might be upon them at any time. But as she began to unpack the Maynards she could not help wondering, did he mean what she thought he meant or was he referring to something entirely different?

Mike returned before there was any sign of the posse. For once he had good news.

'There's a pass that runs directly through the hills. To one side of it there's a box canyon. We could hide in it and hope the posse stick to the main pass. Even if they didn't there's a rock fall near its entrance that looks narrow enough to defend.'

'But Mike, you said there were at least six of them. How could we stand that many off?' asked Polly.

'We couldn't. Or at least we must make the posse think so, then they might get careless enough to give us the chance to even up the odds against us. I have a plan that might just do the trick but it would mean putting Polly into the line of fire,' said Jeff.

'No. I won't let you put Polly into danger. It's me they are after, so it's only fair that I should be the one to take any risks,' said Clara.

'For my plan to work, it has to be Polly and Mike who first greet our pursuers while we keep out of sight. Let me explain,' said Jeff.

CHAPTER FIFTEEN

FIGHT AT
THE PASS

The narrow box canyon was at right angles to the main pass and curved away from it in a gentle arc until it widened out into a clearing at the foot of cliffs so sheer that not even a mountain goat could have climbed them. Although the clearing was completely out of sight of the main pass, hiding in it was not part of Jeff's plan. Nevertheless, he drove the odd-looking wagon and the cayuse horses into the clearing and tethered the Indian-bred animals so they could not work their way back to the main pass.

Mike followed Jeff's wagon into the entrance of the box canyon but stopped the prairie schooner after about a hundred paces by an outcrop of rocks, or perhaps they were boulders that had fallen from the top of the cliff side. After dismounting, he unhitched the horses and then led them into the clearing, where they too were tethered for their own protection. After that he returned to Polly in the prairie wagon to wait for their pursuers. Jeff, carrying the other Maynards, and Clara, carrying as much extra ammunition as she could, followed him. However, neither climbed into the prairie schooner.

They didn't have to wait long. Eight riders swept past the entrance to the box canyon then, espying the rear of the prairie schooner, stopped and turned. But only seven rode into the box canyon. The former deputy sheriff of Clantonville remained in the pass out of sight of the schooner. He knew Clara Marston to be both an intelligent and resourceful spy. Not for a second did he think she would allow herself to be so easily trapped in the back of a prairie schooner. He rightly suspected it was a decoy. Unfortunately for his companions, to further his own ends, he was the sort of man to happily allow his comrades to ride into the trap without warning them.

Drury, however, was not that reckless. He rode into the mouth of the box canyon, then about eighty paces in front of the prairie schooner signalled his men to stop.

'You in the prairie schooner, show yourselves or we open fire!' he yelled.

The canvas awnings at the back of the prairie schooner were suddenly flung open to reveal Mike crouching behind the stout wooden tailboard. He was holding the muzzle-loading, single shot, Springfield musket.

'Mr Drury, what brings you here?' he asked.

'You know damned well,' snarled Drury. 'We want the female Confederate spy travelling with you.'

'But the only woman with me in the prairie schooner is

142

Polly. Surely you've known her too long to believe she's a spy?'

At this, Polly who was lying almost prone, peeped over the tailboard.

'Then I'll take her instead,' said Drury, more calmly than he actually felt.

'You will have to get past me first,' replied Mike.

'There are seven of us and you have just one musket. It takes over three minutes to reload. So how are you going to stop us?'

'I assure you that you will be stopped. Take my advice; turn around and ride out of this canyon. Go home, Mr Drury, while you can.'

It was advice Drury was not about to take. With the odds seemingly overwhelmingly in his favour, he ordered his men to charge.

Eighty paces or less was point-blank range for the Springfield musket. Mike fired. The force of the bullet's impact lifted the rider next to Drury out of his saddle and he crashed to the ground.

The riders galloped on, secure in the knowledge that their adversary would not be able to reload his musket before they overwhelmed him. Indeed, the odds were so heavily in their favour they felt he had little chance against them even if he used his six-gun.

But Mike did not resort to his six-gun; the range was too great. Instead, Polly thrust a loaded Maynard rifle into his hands. This time his bullet struck Drury in the chest. Simultaneously, from behind the rocks alongside the prairie schooner, Jeff opened fire using the first of his stack of Maynard rifles.

As soon as Mike and Jeff fired, the girls handed them another loaded Maynard, giving the oncoming riders the feeling they faced far more men than they actually did.

Desperately, the survivors tried to wheel their horses around. In this they were impeded by the narrow canyon mouth, the bodies of fallen comrades and their riderless horses. By the time they had completed their manoeuvres and started the short journey back to the mouth of the canyon, Mike and Jeff had each reloaded one of their Maynards. Neither missed with their next shots. Only one rider made it safely out of the box canyon. He confronted the former deputy sheriff of Clantonville.

'I thought you said we were chasing one man and maybe a woman. There was about a bloody dozen of them in the box canyon,' he said angrily.

'I guess it's the Reb outfit that attacked the train. Maybe they haven't heard the war is over,' said the former deputy sheriff of Clantonville.

'Whoever they are, I am not going to tangle with them again,' said the other rider. 'I'm heading back to Clantonville.'

'Good idea. I'd ride with you but someone has to warn the garrison at Innocence that there's a Reb outfit still fighting the war.'

Of course, that was just an excuse for the former deputy not to return to Clantonville. He was not at all troubled by the death of his comrades. Indeed, that made his task much simpler. It was the key around Clara's neck he wanted but it was no good to him unless he knew the whereabouts of whatever it was that it opened. He spurred his horse and headed towards Innocence, but the sound of a bugle caused him to rein in and hide behind an outcrop of rock.

A small band of troopers raced past without seeing him and then turned into the box canyon. Mike recognized their leader instantly; it was the lieutenant he had saved during the massacre at the Dawson ranch.

'Welcome, Lieutenant Brown, even if you're a little late, I reckon we've done your work for you,' he said.

'Major Hancock, General Lee has surrendered, the war is over. But what happened here? I think you have some explaining to do.'

'It's a long story, but we have two women with us, so can we first deal with the corpses?'

'Of course, sir. Corporal, see to it.'

It was time for the truth. While the troopers buried the bodies, Mike introduced the lieutenant to Jeff and the women and then related all the relevant incidents since the train crash.

Lieutenant Brown looked suitably shocked but, perhaps because of his West Point training, he rallied quickly.

'No, sir. It won't do. The truth once known will open a can of worms. Bound to be a military enquiry and a court martial for me. Then it will be the gallows for Lieutenant Kyle, prison for you and maybe the firing squad for Miss Marston. You will take direction from me in this matter. Kindly hitch up your wagons and be ready to leave as soon as my men have buried the bodies. I must confer with my corporal.'

An hour later, Lieutenant Brown returned. He had a plan.

'Mr Avison, for the time being you will continue to impersonate Major Hancock. Our story is that you were escorting your companions to Innocence when the Rebs jumped you. By chance we happened along, engaged and killed the Rebs. Once my superiors have accepted my story you will be free to go on your way.'

'Lieutenant, will your troopers support your story?' asked Clara.

'You can depend on it, Miss. They are desperate to go home but my fake report about the Reb troops massacring my command at the Dawson ranch means we won't be disbanded until the rest of the supposed Reb force is captured.'

Escorted by the Union troops, Innocence was reached without further incident. Lieutenant Brown was correct about his troops. To a man they backed his story of the events in the box canyon. Of course, there were formalities to complete and these took time; time that Clara used to send a telegram to her aunt and then to search for the pro-Confederate bank in which was stored the chest that only her key could open. In this task she was not successful, the only bank she could find was one that had unequivocally supported the Union. Besides, it was far larger than the one that had been described to her.

Mike, still posing as Major Hancock, submitted his resignation from the Union Army. The request was not only deferred but, much to Polly's dismay, he was required to live in the garrison's headquarters. However, her dismay turned to joy when he proposed and together they began to make preparations for the wedding. There was another plus for the happy couple, being stationed at the garrison , meant that Mike was not only entitled to full Army pay but also to the back pay owing to the real Major Hancock.

Jeff was kept busy selling the wagons and the Shire horses. There was no shortage of bidders. During the war the Union Army had seized most of the town's supply of wagons and the mighty Shires had many admirers. They were all sorry to let the magnificent horses go but the money they fetched far exceeded their expectations and easily covered the cost of buying meals as well as the price of staying at the hotel for as long as they needed. The deserters' horses taken from the Dawson ranch were returned to the Army.

Clara then received a telegram from her aunt. Apart from the expressions of delight at finding out her niece had survived the war it contained news that could, under certain conditions, be life changing not just for Clara but for all three of her companions. But for the moment, she kept the good news to herself and continued to search for the old bank.

She stumbled across it by sheer chance. She had wandered into a run-down and little used part of Innocence and, a little lost, turned into what appeared to be an alleyway leading towards the hotel at which she, Polly and Jeff were staying. Instead it veered away and then led to what had once been a Southern-backed centre of commerce but was now a series of derelict buildings, and one of them proved to be the bank she had been looking for.

Clara's information had been correct after all, it was just a little out of date. For several months before the outbreak of the Civil War the little bank had actually been a cover for Confederate covert activities. Its manager co-

ordinated the activities of a large number of key undercover Confederate spies working deep in the heart of
Union territory and continued to do so for the first year of
the war. Then its covert activities had been discovered by
Union agents.

Its manager had been shot for acting as a spy and the
rest of the staff imprisoned. The little bank had then been
closed down by Union forces and boarded up to prevent it
being used again. Since then, the rest of the wooden struc-
ture had been allowed to fall into such disrepair that it
now looked more like a derelict barn than a bank.
Situated in such a run-down part of the town, it was little
wonder it had been so difficult to find.

The boarding over the windows and doors at the front
of the bank had recently been renewed, making entry
impossible. Clara ought to have gone back to the hotel to
get Mike and Jeff before even thinking about trying to
enter the little bank but a mixture of frustration at being
so near to the mysterious chest and her natural curiosity
got the better of her. So she decided to walk down the alley
between the side of the old bank and what looked like
some sort of deserted store house to see if there was some
way she could get in. Even if she found one, she wouldn't
actually go inside. No, of course not; it was more that Jeff
might be more impressed with her if she had found a way.

The alleyway opened out into a small square bounded
on all sides by what looked like disused buildings. There
was not a soul in sight. Indeed, judging by its derelict
appearance it looked as if no one had visited the square
for a long time. No one except for a large crow-like bird,
which had been sleeping inside the bank. Startled by

Clara's sudden appearance, it let out a rasping call of alarm and made its escape through a broken window shutter and then flew rapidly away.

The broken window shutter had a hole in it easily large enough for Clara to climb through. Without even looking around to see if she was alone, she clambered through it, making a fair amount of noise as she did so.

She stumbled and almost fell. Unlike the once imposing front of the bank, the back part of the bank had not only been open to the elements for a considerable time it had been built cheaply using low-quality materials. Consequently, some of the floor boards were so rotten that parts of them had collapsed, leaving several gaping holes. A beam of sunlight shone through one of them, revealing that below the floorboards was a large crypt-like vault.

There was a door on the opposite side of the bank floor. Gingerly, Clara walked towards it. The floor creaked and groaned as she carefully walked around the holes. To her surprise, it was not locked. A rickety staircase led down to the vault. Without any sort of lantern she should not have gone down but, of course, she did. She was too near to finding the chest to give up now.

Pools of light shining through the holes in the bank floor broke through the darkness of the rest of the vault. Slowly, Clara's eyes grew accustomed to the gloom. Dust was almost everywhere and yet she was certain that somebody had visited the vault quite recently. It seemed that a pile of chests had been opened quite recently because there was little dust on the papers in them. Fortunately, none of the open ones was the chest she was looking for. It took her ten minutes of scrambling to find the one her key fitted. Not only was it much older and larger than she had expected, the brass lock was stiff from lack of use.

The trunk was thick with dust, so first she cleaned around the lock using the hem of her skirt. It didn't make the lock any easier to open but after a struggle she managed it. Much to her consternation, the chest contained not one list but layer after layer of papers and parchments, some of them looking really old. However, the vault was far too gloomy to examine them. She relocked the chest and tried to lift it but it was so heavy she couldn't get it off the ground. So what lay hidden under the piles of papers that weighed so much? She was about to reopen it to find out when the boards forming the ceiling began to creak and groan and then she heard the sounds of footsteps directly above her.

She returned the key to her necklace, replaced it around her neck and then tucked it under her blouse. For no good reason, she then buttoned her blouse right up to her neck.

The door at the top of the stairs suddenly swung open. A lantern illuminated the top of the stairs but its light was not strong enough to penetrate all the gloom of the vault. Taking care to avoid the pools of half-light pouring through the holes in the ceiling, Clara tiptoed to another pile of boxes and crouched behind them.

It was not a moment too soon. The holder of the lantern began to descend, almost stumbling on the rickety staircase as he did so. He swore angrily. Clara recognized the voice instantly; it was the deputy sheriff from Clantonville.

After searching around for a few minutes, he found the

trunk Clara had opened. He couldn't fail to see that the area around the lock had been recently disturbed. After checking it was still locked, he transferred his lantern to his left hand, drew his six-gun and began to search the vault floor. It didn't take him long to discover Clara's hiding place.

'Come out of there, Miss Marston. I've been tracking you ever since you and your friends hit town. If you give me the key to the trunk without any fuss, you have my word that no harm will come to you. All I want is the contents of the chest.'

Of course, Clara didn't believe him. They were in an unused vault under a long-closed bank situated in the most deserted part of town, so who would hear a pistol shot, she thought swiftly.

'Do you think I'd be stupid enough to carry the key on me? It's in the hotel's safe.'

Of course, it was a lie. The key was still attached to the necklace hidden under her blouse.

'You don't fool me,' the former deputy snarled. 'Why would you be in the bank's vault if you couldn't open whatever it is you're looking for? So let's go back outside where the light is better and I can see if you are wearing the key on your necklace.'

Silently she cursed herself. Had she been more patient and gone back to the hotel to get Jeff before searching the bank vault she might not be in this mess. She needn't have worried. Jeff, dressed in civilian clothes, was standing in the square waiting for them as they clambered through the broken shutter. But the former deputy's six-gun was already drawn and he pointed it at Clara's temple. His other arm was clamped so tightly around her waist she could not move.

'Stop right there and let the lady go, deputy,' he said.

'I might do that except my six-gun is drawn and yours is not. So unbuckle your gunbelt and let it drop to the ground.'

'Maybe it is. But it's pointed at the lady's head and not at me. So tell the lady to remove the key we both want from her necklace and give it to me.'

As he spoke, Jeff moved to his left, which, of course, was to the deputy's right. That meant the deputy would have to swing his six-gun, still pointing at Clara's temple, in a great arc to his right before he could get a bead on his adversary. Jeff knew that was all the time he needed to outdraw the deputy.

However, the deputy stood his ground.

'Even if you get me with your first shot, I'd still kill your lady friend. So I think I still have the advantage,' he said.

'I'd sure be sorry about that. But then, the money in the chest would buy me enough saloon girls to make me happy again.'

Even though she knew Jeff was only bluffing, Clara blanched at his harsh words. Then, while the men were arguing and trying to stare each other down, she caught the glint of a rifle barrel. It came from the shadowy alley leading back to the main town. In a blink it was gone. Had it been a signal to her or had the deputy sheriff, to cover his back, left one of his cronies in the alley? There was no way she could tell. Nevertheless, she formed a dangerous and daring plan.

Try as hard as she could, she could not break the iron

152

grip of the deputy's arm around her waist. So instead of continuing to struggle she did the opposite and pretended to faint. She deliberately buckled at the knees and slumped into a jackknife over the deputy's arm still firmly clasped around her waist. Indeed, her hands touched her boots and her long raven-coloured hair fell down in front of her eyes, partially obscuring her vision.

The deputy, taken by surprised by the sudden weight imposed on his left arm, staggered. As he did so, his gun hand wavered and his shot missed its target. It was the chance Jeff had been waiting for. He fired; almost simultaneously another shot rang out. Clara felt no pain as she plummeted to the ground but then the black pit of oblivion opened up and engulfed her.

CHAPTER SIXTEEN

WHITE LIES

As she slowly regained consciousness, Clara found she was again supported by a pair of arms wrapped firmly around her waist. But this time they belonged to Jeff. Still groggy after her fall when the deputy had been killed, she cuddled into him.

'Easy now. You're safe; I've got hold of you,' said Jeff.

She felt so safe in his arms, she didn't want him to let go and that seemed to be more than alright with him. Then Mike intervened.

'Sorry to break up you two love birds but by the sound of it we got company.'

Mike was right. From the shadowy alley that ran alongside the old bank came the sound of horses' hoofs. Suddenly, Lieutenant Brown, followed by six troopers, galloped into the square. He dismounted, ordered his troopers to do the same and then surveyed the scene.

The lifeless body of the deputy lay sprawled on the

ground. Jeff had left it there after lifting it off Clara as she lay unconscious on the ground. The deputy's wrist had been shattered by Mike's skilfully aimed shot. He had trailed Jeff into the alley but remained hidden in the shadows in order to cover Jeff's back. While the deputy's attention had been temporarily distracted by Jeff, Mike had deliberately thrust the barrel of his rifle into the sunlight hoping that Clara would see it and cause a diversion to allow him a clear shot at the deputy's gun hand. However, it had been Jeff's shot, straight between the deputy's eyes, that had killed him instantly.

'Anyone care to explain?' asked the lieutenant.

'He was the deputy sheriff of Clantonville and he was after me,' said Clara, reluctantly disentangling herself from Jeff's arms. He too seemed reluctant to let go.

'But he has no jurisdiction here. So why would he be chasing you?' asked the lieutenant.

Clara, tired of running and sickened by the carnage her secret had caused, decided to tell the truth.

'I have a key to a chest in the old bank vault. The deputy thought it was full of money but I was told it contained documents listing. . . .'

'You have the key?' interrupted Lieutenant Brown hastily. He did not want his troopers to overhear Clara incriminate herself. His previous action and statements to his superiors would then be brought into question and thus make his situation untenable. He had to take charge of the situation; courts martial and a lengthy prison sentence would be his fate if his earlier false statements came to light.

'Miss Marston, the key if you please.'

In truth, Clara was glad to be rid of it. From the moment she had been given the key she had witnessed all the bloodshed and carnage she could stomach. On the other hand, without the key, she might not have met Jeff.

The lieutenant took the key and addressed the man he knew to be Mike Avison.

'Major Hancock, will you be so good as to escort Miss Marston and her companion back to their hotel and ensure they do not leave town until this matter has been thoroughly investigated? Of course, I shall have to report my findings to my superiors, so it may be a few days before I get further instructions.'

However, it didn't take days, it took weeks, during which time, in the traditional way, wedding banns for the marriage of Mike and Polly were called at the local church. It was to be a simple ceremony with Jeff acting as the best man and Clara playing the role of maid of honour. After the one and only rehearsal, Jeff followed Clara and when they were alone started to ask her about her future plans.

'I suppose you will be going back east to live with your aunt as soon as the lieutenant sorts out the contents of your mysterious chest treasure chest?'

'Maybe. Would you miss me?' she said, blushing profusely.

'Yes. If things were different I'd. . . .' Jeff broke off his voice choked with emotion but rallied quickly and continued. 'As it is I'm a wanted man. I have just enough money left to buy provisions to head west and then ride across Texas to New Mexico.'

'Why New Mexico? Why not Texas?' asked Clara.

'Because New Mexico is a territory, not an official US state, so Federal law would have no jurisdiction over me. Once there, although I'd be a free man, I'd have no money left so would have to start from scratch.'

Although Jeff had not actually said so, Clara had her answer; he cared for her. It was just he was too much of a gentleman to expect her to face the wilderness of the Texas Panhandle and then the hardship in starting a new life in the New Mexico Territories. Nevertheless, there was still one piece of the jigsaw left to find before she could reveal the plan she had for their future, so she just smiled and changed the subject.

That missing jigsaw piece came to light the next morning when Lieutenant Brown summoned Clara to his office. They were locked in private talks for more than an hour before agreement was reached. That agreement had to be ratified at the highest level, so the telegraph line between Innocence and Washington was kept busy for the rest of the day.

Next day they were all summoned to the lieutenant's office. Except his new tunic showed he was no longer a lieutenant of the old Union Army but a captain in the newly formed US Cavalry. On his desk were four affidavits and on the floor by it was the chest from the old bank vault. Captain Brown got straight down to business.

'Please sign these statements. To save you wading through a load of legal waffle, I will read the important details. Clara Marston, an undercover agent for the Union, infiltrated a powerful Confederate spy organisation and learned of a dangerous contingency plan should the South be forced to surrender.

'She discovered these plans were stored in a bank in Innocence. Having gotten hold of the key, with the aid of Major Hancock, they escaped but were then pursued by a Reb outfit. In an attempt to throw them off their trail they joined forces with you two,' Captain Brown pointed at Polly and Geoff.

'But there's not a word of truth in it. Surely the authorities will investigate and find out,' protested Polly.

Captain Brown did not answer her. Instead, he opened the chest and with some difficulty pulled out a small but very heavy canvas bag and carefully tipped it up. Hundreds of strange-looking gold coins cascaded on to his desk.

'There will be no investigation,' said the captain, and then seeing the puzzled look on his fellow conspirators' faces, began to explain.

'They're English gold sovereigns and just a fraction of the hoard we found hidden in the old bank vault. All paperwork, including the list of Confederate agents, has been burnt. The sovereigns will be secretly shipped to Washington, where they will be melted down and turned into gold ingots. Britain can't admit they were part financing a rebellion against the rightful government of the USA, so as long as we all keep to the same story the matter will be closed.

'Although your discharge has been agreed, Mike, you will have to continue to be Major Hancock, otherwise the story won't hold up to any scrutiny. The good news is that Washington has decreed that Miss Clara is entitled to a substantial reward for her help in recovering the gold.'

Affidavits signed, Clara addressed the meeting.

'I have already used most of the reward money to